Mixing It

Rosemary Hayes

F

FRANCES LINCOLN
CHILDREN'S BOOKS

Mixing It

My thanks to Maria Aboukhshem
and members of the Al-Noor Girls' Group
for answering all my questions and for
checking the typescript of this book

Mixing It copyright © Frances Lincoln Limited 2007
Text copyright © Rosemary Hayes 2007

First published in Great Britain in 2007 by
Frances Lincoln Children's Books, 4 Torriano Mews,
Torriano Avenue, London NW5 2RZ
www.franceslincoln.com

British Library Cataloguing in Publication Data available on request

ISBN: 978-184507-495-1

Set in New Baskerville and Stone Sans Italic

Printed in the UK by CPI Bookmarque, Croydon, CR0 4TD

3 5 7 9 8 6 4 2

'It is better to light a candle
than to curse the darkness.'

Chinese proverb

Note: 'Uncle' and 'Auntie' are used by young Muslims as terms of respect for their elders, whether they are related or not.

CHAPTER ONE

'STEVE!'

Mum's voice drifted up the stairs. Steve heard her – just – but took no notice. He pulled the duvet over his head to block out the morning light.

Somewhere in his subconscious he heard her climb the stairs, come into his bedroom and cross the floor to his bed. He knew there'd only be a few more seconds' peace.

Now she was leaning over him, shaking him.

'Come on, love. You'll be late.' Her voice was weary.

Steve grunted but didn't move.

With a practised flick of the wrist, Mum twitched the duvet right off the bed and on to the floor.

'ARRRH!

Mum's face came close to his. 'I really don't need this, Steve. I shouldn't still be having to dig you out of bed every morning. You're seventeen, for goodness sake. You should be getting yourself up and off to school on time!'

'I set the alarm, didn't I? Can't help it if I didn't hear it,' muttered Steve, slowly heaving his legs over the edge of the bed. His blue eyes were bleary with sleep and his sandy eyebrows were drawn together in a scowl. He rubbed his eyes with his fists. 'It's orright, Mum. I'm awake.'

She smiled but didn't move.

'Mum, for Chrissake leave me alone. I'm getting up, right?'

She said nothing. Just waited.

Very slowly, Steve stood up, swaying slightly.

At last she turned and walked out of the room.

Steve stretched, yawned and blinked. Gradually his bedroom swam into focus. The footie posters, posters of his favourite band, the desk with an untidy heap of books, DVDs and papers, his laptop and a chair laden with clothes.

He staggered over to the window and looked out. It was an ordinary sort of day, cloudy and muggy. Hardly worth getting up for, he thought. He ran his hands through his tousled mop of fair hair and rubbed one large foot on the back of the other leg.

'Ow!' he said out loud. He must remember to cut his toenails.

Then, hopefully, he felt his chin but there was still no sign of proper stubble. He made a brief visit to the bathroom and then came back and stared at his clothes. He picked up one sock and sniffed it. Not too bad. He truffled around until he found it a friend; this one smelt worse, but he knew there weren't any clean ones. Mum refused to wash anything unless he put it in the laundry basket, and somehow his dirty clothes hardly ever made it to the laundry basket.

He dragged on his crumpled school trousers, pushed his feet into his shoes, found a half-clean shirt to wear and then stuffed all his books into his school bag. Still half-asleep, he clumped down the stairs and into the kitchen.

Mum was shrugging her arms into her jacket. She buttoned it and then took a moment to brush off imaginary hairs and glance quickly in the mirror.

Steve's Dad was sitting at the kitchen table finishing his breakfast and reading the paper.

Mum bent down and dropped a quick kiss on his head.

'Have a good day,' she said.

Dad glanced up at her. 'You too, love. And Jackie ...'

'Yes?'

'Don't go working too hard, will you?'

She shook her head, then blew a kiss to Steve and went out.

Dad watched her go. 'Your mum's looking really tired,' he said.

Steve said nothing. If she left him alone and stopped nagging him, perhaps she wouldn't get so tired, he thought crossly. And then immediately he felt guilty. She did work hard. She had a better job than his dad and she earned more, but she never, ever put his dad down.

Steve knew she nagged because she worried about him. She wanted him to get a good job, not a dead end one like his dad. That's why he'd stayed on at school, wasn't it? For her. That's why he was going to take his A-levels. He'd wanted to leave school last year and if he'd had his way, he'd be out earning money by now.

Still standing, he grabbed a piece of toast and swore under his breath when a globule of marmalade landed on his shirt front. He scraped it off with a knife, then took a gulp from the mug of tea that Mum had poured out for him.

Suddenly Dad snorted and jabbed his finger at the newspaper. 'Damn Muslims,' he said.

Steve frowned. 'What?'

'Another bombing. Another terrorist bombing.'

'Oh yeah. Where's that?'

'In Manchester.'

'Oh.' Steve wasn't really listening. He was thinking about the course work he hadn't done – and about going to the town centre with his friends at lunchtime.

Dad threw down the paper and thumped the table with his fist. 'I don't know why we ever let them in, all these extremists. They cause nothing but trouble. They take advantage of everything we have to offer and now they're trying to ruin our way of life. I tell you, son, they'll take us over.'

Steve had heard this rant before. 'Aw, come on, Dad,' he said mildly. 'Not every British Muslim is an extremist!'

'British Muslims! British! This immigration lark is madness.'

Steve wanted to stay and argue, though he knew he'd have no chance of changing his dad's views. And, in any case, he was late. He glanced at his watch. Hell, he really was late!

Dad got up and turned on the kitchen telly. There were pictures of devastation, with a young woman reporter talking to camera. Ambulances screamed in the background.

Steve looked at it briefly. He'd seen it all before.

He stuffed the last bit of toast into his mouth, slurped down the rest of his tea and heaved his school bag on to his back.

'Gotta go, Dad! See you.'

Dad grunted and raised his hand but didn't take his eyes off the television.

Steve ran all the way to the bus stop, his stomach objecting strongly to the sudden activity. He got there just in time to see the bus pulling away and turning the corner.

He'd never catch the bus now and he'd have to wait ages for another.

He'd have to leg it. He'd done it often enough before. If he really motored, he could get there before the first lesson.

He bent over and took some deep breaths to ease the stitch in his side, and then he set off. It was OK. He'd make it. He knew all the short cuts through the side streets. But it was a real pain. It was going to be a BAD day.

G G G

No one noticed the young man shrugging off his backpack as he inched his way round the building and into the dark of the church porch. As he entered, he looked up briefly but he knew there were no surveillance cameras here.

It was done in an instant. Then he was away, just as quietly as he had come.

Across town, in a house near the school, Fatimah was going through her morning routine.

Her parents had always told her that the beginning of the day should be a peaceful time, but it wasn't easy when she'd been up late revising. It was tempting to lie in bed a bit longer – like her brother, Hassan, who left everything to the last possible minute.

She said a familiar line from the Koran: 'It is Allah who made your dwellings homes of rest and quiet for you.'

There was a knock on her bedroom door. It was her mother.

'The bathroom's free, Fatimah. You can wash now.'

Fatimah padded into the bathroom. Washing before praying wasn't just a matter of face and teeth. She had to do *wudu*, the ritual washing of hands, mouth, nose, face, arms, head, ears, neck and feet three times each in running water.

Fatimah turned on the tap and began her washing. She enjoyed it. It calmed her and prepared her for the day ahead.

Her faith was part of her. She lived and breathed it as naturally as the air about her. From early childhood she had been taught the rules to be obeyed, and they were good and sensible rules.

Some of her Muslim girlfriends came from more liberal families, families which had become very Westernised. Some of them didn't do *salah* – the five daily prayers – or even go to the mosque regularly. And many of them no longer wore the *hijab*, the headscarf, when they were outside.

But it doesn't make them happy, thought Fatimah. It confuses them. They don't know where they belong.

Yet being a British Muslim did mean making some changes. All over the world, the Muslim faith was the same: the beliefs were the same, but there were different customs for every culture.

Since coming to Britain, Fatimah's family had adapted. Although her parents still rose at sunrise to make the first prayer of the day, going back to bed afterwards, no one expected Fatimah or Hassan to do this. They made their first prayer of the day as soon as they got up. At least, Fatimah did. She suspected that Hassan didn't do much praying at all.

During the month of Ramadan, though, the whole family rose at sunrise to eat, because for the rest of the day they would eat and drink nothing at all. Nothing until sunset, when they would break their fast with a big meal. Fatimah loved Ramadan. There was lots of socialising between Muslim families.

Often they would have their friends over for the evening meal, or go visiting.

There were a lot of Muslims at Fatimah's school and there was a place set aside for prayer, but if the prayer times clashed with lessons, it was impossible to get away. And the prayer times changed every day, depending on when the sun rose and set. Sometimes it just wasn't possible to pray at the right times during the day, so two sets of prayers were said together. And you didn't have to do wudu before each prayer time, so long as you'd not got dirty since the last prayers.

Fatimah finished her washing. As she was drying her face, she looked in the mirror. She had an oval face and big dark eyes framed by a mass of lustrous black hair. She wasn't vain, but she knew she wasn't bad-looking. Some of the young men in her community looked at her differently now and she enjoyed their attention, but she was glad that she had the hijab to protect her from some of the other male stares out in the street.

She was sixteen and having to think about her future, make decisions about the AS and A levels she would take. She desperately wanted to be a doctor, but she wasn't sure that she was clever enough.

She knew that her mother and father wanted her to do well at school but she knew they worried about her, too. They were so frightened that she would come under bad influences and lose her faith. They were so over-protective!

But today, it was Fatimah who was feeling protective. She was really worried about Zahrah, one of her girlfriends. She couldn't believe it: Zahrah had agreed to go clubbing with a non-Muslim boy at the weekend. Clubbing was absolutely off-limits for Muslim girls and Fatimah had tried to reason with her.

'You don't know what you're letting yourself in for,' she'd said. 'All the boys will think you're fast. And your dad's sure to find out.'

Zahrah had just shrugged and told her to loosen up. But Fatimah had persisted.

'What will your father say?'

'I'm not going to tell him – and nor will you, Fatimah, if you know what's good for you. And in any case, my family's much more liberal than yours. It's not such a big deal for us.'

Fatimah couldn't understand why Zahrah would want to date a non-Muslim boy. No non-Muslim could really understand where Muslim girls were coming from. And whatever Zahrah said, Fatimah knew that her family would be furious if they found out. And someone would be bound to tell them.

From an early age, Muslim girls were taught the importance of modesty, particularly outside the home. Any demonstration of public affection – kissing, holding hands in public – was disapproved of. And they were never allowed to drink alcohol, or to be in a place where alcohol was served. Nor were Muslim boys, for that matter, though she suspected that many of the male Muslim students probably hung around the bar at college.

Fatimah's parents, like all good Muslim parents, disapproved of many of the programmes on television and whenever there was anything vulgar shown, or any swearing, they would switch off or turn to another channel. Fatimah followed their example. She didn't want to be made to feel awkward and uncomfortable.

She went back to her bedroom. She dressed in *salwaar kameez* – long trousers and a modest, long-sleeved top, then brushed her black hair until it shone. She arranged her hijab round her head and neck, put her prayer mat on the floor and stood in front of it in the first prayer position, her hands up on either side of her head.

Fatimah said the Arabic prayers and assumed the different praying positions with ease. Ever since she was four years old, she'd attended the *madrasah*, the special school at the mosque, where she'd learnt to read and write Arabic and to recite from the Koran. She had always loved the sound of the words from the Koran; their rhythm made a song in her head.

At the end of the set prayer, Fatimah stayed kneeling for a little longer than usual, adding her own private prayer. She prayed for strength to resist temptation, to respect her parents, to work hard and to be true to her faith. And she prayed that Allah would change Zahrah's mind.

She put her prayer mat away and looked at her watch. It was getting late. She ran downstairs and into the kitchen. Her father and mother were already there, but there was no sign of Hassan.

A moment later, Hassan came tumbling down the stairs and took his place at the table, which was set with cereals and fruit juice, toast and yoghurt. Fatimah's mum poured out tea for them all, but no one started to eat until the whole family had said *Bismillah-ir Rahman-ir-Rahim* ('In the name of Allah All-Gracious All-Merciful').

'Hassan, don't gobble!' said his father. 'Enjoy your food. There is no rush.'

'Sorry Dad,' Hassan said, 'I'm starving,' and he grinned across at Fatimah.

Fatimah smiled back. Hassan was a model son at home, but outside it was another story. He was at university in the town and had a lot of freedom. He was spreading his wings and relishing all that student life had to offer. He had more freedom than

18

she would ever be allowed, and no one questioned him about his comings and goings. And since he had become so much freer, he had, perversely, become really protective of her, as if he was more aware than ever, now, of the dangers she faced as a Muslim girl. He was beginning to behave like a second father!

His voice broke into her thoughts. 'What's happening at school today, little sister?'

Fatimah made a face at him. 'What do you think? Course work to finish, mock GCSEs to get through.'

Her father patted Fatimah's hand. 'You're a good student, Fatimah.'

Fatimah blushed. He didn't often praise her.

She stood up and started to help her mother clear the table. She stacked the dishes in the dishwasher and then got ready for school. She kissed her mother goodbye and went to say goodbye to her father and Hassan, who were talking in the lounge.

Her father was pointing at something in the newspaper. He was looking very angry.

'Fools!' he muttered.

'What is it?' asked Fatimah.

Hassan shrugged. 'Another bombing,' he said.

'And are they saying the same things?' asked Fatimah.

Her father nodded. 'Muslim extremists thought to be responsible,' he said, reading the headline.

'And we all know what that means for us,' said Hassan grimly.

Fatimah knew only too well. More insults thrown at her in the street. Would it ever end?

She drew her hijab more tightly round her face and then let herself out of the front door.

CHAPTER TWO

Fatimah passed the house next door and waved towards the window. There was an answering wave from her grandmother, who watched her go by each morning. Then she walked on down the road and turned left into a smaller street. At one of the houses, she stopped and knocked tentatively on the door.

There was silence for a couple of minutes, then the familiar crashing and banging, shouts of goodbye, wrenching open of the front door, and her best friend, Aisha, came tumbling out, hijab awry, school bag half-open, and a huge grin on her face.

They were so different, these two girls, yet the friendship between them was very strong. Fatimah often wished she could be more like Aisha. Aisha was completely open about her faith. She took everyone on, arguing her case with wit and humour. She was a clever girl and she was never apologetic about being a Muslim. She demanded respect, and most of the time she got it.

Aisha grabbed hold of Fatimah's arm, gave it a squeeze, and together they walked towards school.

'What are we going to do about Zahrah?' said Aisha as they walked along the street.

'What can we do? She's headstrong – like you. If she's decided to go clubbing, she'll probably go!'

'Huh!' said Aisha. 'She's not at all like me! I may be headstrong, but I'm not stupid! She's being so stupid. And she's weak. She just wants to be accepted by Craig and his friends.'

Fatimah nodded. 'She's trying to be something she isn't,' she said. 'No one will respect her for it. Craig won't, nor will his friends. And as for her family ...'

Aisha raised her eyes to the leaden sky. 'If her family find out! Can you imagine? No decent Muslim boy will have anything to do with her if he knows she's been clubbing.'

'We must stop her,' said Fatimah. 'You speak to her again, Aisha. She listens to you.'

'No she doesn't! I've talked myself hoarse and she doesn't take a blind bit of notice.'

They were silent for a moment, then Fatimah said slowly. 'I think she's too scared to back down. I don't think she wants to go at all really, but she's dug herself into a hole and she can't get out without losing face.'

Aisha frowned. 'Hmm. Could be. Tell you what,' she went on. 'Why don't we go and talk to Craig – explain to him what damage it would do if he took her clubbing? He hasn't a clue. He doesn't know what the rest of us will think of her if she goes.'

'D'you think we should interfere?'

'Yes,' said Aisha firmly. 'Craig's OK. He just doesn't understand the pressure he's putting her under.'

'All right,' said Fatimah, reluctantly. 'I suppose. If it's going to help Zahrah.'

'We'll try and speak to him before the first lesson.'

Fatimah nodded. But she wasn't very happy at the prospect. She changed the subject.

'How is Uncle Ismail getting on?'

'He's arrived in Jeddah. We had an email yesterday.'

Ismail was making the *hajj* – the pilgrimage to Mecca in Saudi Arabia. All Muslims tried to make the pilgrimage once in their lives, if possible. The pilgrimage happened every year – during the last month of the Muslim year – and all those on the pilgrimage would celebrate the feast of Eid-ul-Adha at the camp at Mina, near Mecca. And all the Muslims not going on the pilgrimage – those left behind – celebrated at home with family and friends.

'I can't wait for Eid,' said Aisha. 'I think Mum and Dad are finally going to get me a laptop!'

Fatimah grinned. 'I've already got your present,' she said.

'Fantastic. What is it?'

'I'm not telling. Wait and see!'

'Hey,' said Aisha. 'Wouldn't it be great if we could go on the hajj together one day?'

'Do you think we'll ever get there?'

'Of course we will. You'll see.'

'But our parents haven't been yet.'

'They'll go one day. Look at your grandmother. She and your grandad went, didn't they? And they thought they'd never make it.'

Fatimah nodded. Her grandad had fulfilled his ambition and seen Mecca before he died – but only just. And Fatimah's grandmother never stopped telling her about every minute of every day of the pilgrimage. Fatimah almost felt as if she'd been there herself.

They turned the corner into St Luke's Road and the big church of St Luke's, which stood just behind the school, came into view.

Briefly, Fatimah looked up at its huge Victorian brick frontage and high steeple dominating the street. She had never been inside, even though she passed it every day.

☾ ☾ ☾

Safely out of sight, the young man waited and listened.

☾ ☾ ☾

Steve slowed down. He had taken off his jacket, but the straps of his heavy school bag were biting into his shoulders, so he took it off and shrugged it down so that it swung from one hand. He was hot and sweating. The day was muggy and close. He wondered vaguely whether there would be a thunderstorm. He hoped so. It would clear the air.

He dug in his trouser pocket and found a crumpled heap of tissues. He took them out and wiped his forehead. He could kill for a drink, but of course he'd forgotten to bring any water.

He sighed and walked on. The stitch in his side was still there, but he'd made good time and he could walk for the rest of the way.

He looked about him. None of his mates lived in this part of town, but a lot of Muslim families did. He smiled grimly. Not a place where his dad would feel comfortable!

Steve was hungry and wished he'd had more breakfast, but he could always get something from the machine at school. Then he cursed as he remembered that he hadn't got any money with him. Well, maybe he could borrow from someone.

He turned into St Luke's Road.

Ahead of him he saw two Muslim girls. They were walking slowly, chatting together. He vaguely recognised them and thought that they were in the year below him, but he'd never spoken to them. He didn't even know their names.

As they passed in front of the church, Steve began to overtake them.

He looked up at the sky as he passed them, expecting a roll of thunder.

But when the noise came, it wasn't thunder. It was a different, terrifying, deafening noise. It was the noise of a massive explosion, and it was immediately followed by a swift and powerful rush of wind.

Steve was lifted right off his feet. The blast drove him backwards, backwards into the place where once there had stood the imposing main door of the church – and where now there was nothing but a great, dark void. It hurled him, together with a mass of bricks and masonry, broken glass and wooden beams, on to the unyielding stone floor.

He heard screams, but they could have been his own, for, just before his body hit the ground and he lost consciousness, he was aware of an unbearable pain in his leg.

But his weren't the only screams. Fatimah and Aisha had been wrenched apart by the blast. Screaming and flailing, they, too, were blown back, like a couple of rag dolls, into the gaping mouth of the bombed church.

☾ ☾ ☾

It was done. The young man's shoulders relaxed. Quickly and quietly he walked away from the area.

☾ ☾ ☾

At first, there was an eerie silence in St Luke's Road, broken only by the sound of shifting bricks and masonry.

Then people came rushing from nearby houses, staring, pointing at the gaping hole where the front of the church had been, clutching at each other in disbelief.

'Where are those youngsters?' yelled someone. 'There were two girls and a boy walking past the church. I saw them.'

'Yes, I saw them too. They must have been on their way to school,' said another.

Then voices came from everywhere. 'Has anyone phoned 999?'

'Let's get into the rubble. We must find those kids.'

'It's too dangerous. Look at that brickwork. It's going to collapse at any minute. We'll have to wait for the police and ambulance to come.'

☾ ☾ ☾

Fatimah's mother was alone in the house. She was at her computer, dealing with emails connected with the business she ran from home.

When the explosion came, it was so strong that all the windows shook.

She sat there, stunned, for a moment, not moving. Then she hastily put on her hijab and ran out of the front door. Her mother – Fatimah's grandmother – was already outside.

'What is it? What was that dreadful noise?'

There were other people in the street, too. They were pointing at a great plume of smoke rising from a couple of streets away. People started running towards it.

Fatimah's mother muttered prayers under her breath. 'Merciful Allah,' she said, as she ran. 'Let her be unharmed. Don't let my beautiful Fatimah come to harm.'

As she passed Aisha's house, she hesitated. There was no point in knocking. They'd all be gone by now. Or else they'd be hurrying towards that dreadful pall of smoke too.

When she reached St Luke's Road, Fatimah's mother joined the small crowd that had gathered. Her hand flew to her mouth when she saw the damage to the church.

'Was anyone hurt?' she said to the first person she saw.

'I dunno, dear. I've only just got here. Dreadful, isn't it?'

Then she saw a Muslim woman she knew vaguely. She ran over to her. 'Was anyone hurt?'

The woman turned to her. 'Someone said that there were three young people near the church when the blast happened,' she said.

'Were there two Muslim girls?'

The woman shook her head. 'I don't know.'

Someone else overheard them. 'Yes, I think so. They said there were two Muslim girls and a boy.'

Fatimah's mother drew her mobile phone from her pocket and scrolled down until she found the number of the school. She asked if Fatimah and Aisha had arrived.

There was a long wait while the Secretary went to find out. Then at last:

'No, they've not arrived yet.'

'But they should be there.' Her voice was rising.

'They left in plenty of time. Are you sure they're not there?'

'Quite sure... look, there's been an explosion – a bomb at the church round the corner. Everything's chaos.'

'I know,' said Fatimah's mother quietly. 'The girls walk past the church every morning.'

There was a shocked silence, then the Secretary spoke again. 'Oh! Oh, I'm sorry. You don't think... I'm so sorry.' Her voice trailed away.

'Please, if you find out anything,' said Fatimah's mother, trying to keep her voice steady, 'will you phone me on my mobile?'

'Of course. Yes, of course I will.'

CHAPTER THREE

Fatimah groaned. Then she coughed. It was quiet and dark and there was dust everywhere. Although she could hardly see anything, she could feel the dust swirling about her.

She tried to move, but there was a large piece of wood over her legs. It was heavy, but by concentrating all her strength and effort she finally succeeded in shifting it. She felt absurdly pleased with herself.

She tested her legs to make sure she could still move them and then, slowly and carefully, she sat up. Her school bag was still on her back; it must have broken her fall. She slipped it off her shoulders, wincing with pain.

She felt her arms and her legs. They were scraped and bruised and she could feel the warmth and stickiness of blood, but she could move everything.

Nothing broken, then.

Her head was throbbing. She put her hand up and

felt a large swelling. Had she lost consciousness? How long had she been here? She had no idea. The last thing she remembered was chatting to Aisha about presents for Eid.

Aisha! Where was Aisha?

Gradually, Fatimah's eyes became accustomed to the darkness around her and she stared into it.

Until then, she had just been thankful to be alive. Alive and more or less all right. But now she started to panic. How would she get out of here? Would someone find her? And where was Aisha?

'Aisha!' she called into the darkness. Her voice sounded strange to her, hoarse and unnaturally high.

Nothing. No reply.

She could see a little more, now. Her eyes were adjusting. She was under an arch, an arch which was still standing. It must have been this which had protected her from worse injury. But to either side of the arch there was rubble, with choking dust still floating about in what little light was coming in.

'Aisha!' she yelled again.

She waited. Aisha had to be here somewhere, didn't she? They'd been walking along the pavement side by side. She must be nearby. Fatimah didn't dare to breathe as she waited for some response.

She was just about to shout out again when she thought she heard a faint sound. She listened, straining her ears. Had she imagined it?

She kept listening – and then it came again. A feeble moan. It was coming from a little way off, beyond the arch.

Very very carefully, Fatimah started to crawl towards where she thought the noise was coming from. She looked up once – and felt sick with fear. There were crossbeams and shattered brickwork above her. She knew that it could all shift and fall on her at any moment. She didn't dare look up again.

Bit by bit, she inched forward, stopping every now and again to call out and to try and pinpoint the answering moan.

Then she saw it: a scrap of Aisha's scarf, sticking out from under the rubble.

Carefully she started moving the rubble, brick by brick, stone by stone, and all the time whispering encouragement.

'I'm here. I'm coming,' she muttered. 'Hang in there, Aisha. Don't give up. I'm here.'

Her fingers were raw with scrabbling and digging when, at last, she got down to Aisha. Gently, she removed the last bricks and stones.

Aisha lay face down, her arms spread out.

Fatimah was gripped by a cold terror. 'Merciful Allah,' she repeated, again and again. She managed to turn Aisha so that she lay face upwards. Fatimah bent down and listened, but Aisha wasn't breathing.

Fatimah tried to think calmly. 'If you are going to be a doctor, girl, you'd better prove yourself here and now,' she said. She tried to remember the first aid session she'd once been to. *Clear the airway, put into recovery position, give the kiss of life. Cross your hands over the patient's chest; push push push push.* But as she gently lifted Aisha's head, she realised that nothing could help her now. Aisha's head lolled over. Her neck was broken.

Fatimah sat back on her heels and clasped Aisha's hands in hers, tears streaming down her cheeks.

Her lovely, funny, clever, faithful friend. They would never travel to Mecca together now.

Desperately, she tried to remember some of the prayers for the dead. She cast her mind back to her grandad's death. Only the men in the family had been to his burial, so she had not seen him wrapped in the special burial cloths and placed, facing Mecca, in the grave dug in the Muslim plot in the local cemetery, but she had prayed for him, with her mum and dad and Hassan.

She took some deep breaths. She could remember. She must – for Aisha's sake. She must say a prayer over her poor, crushed body.

She released Aisha's hands and put her own hands into the first praying position.

'Merciful Allah,' she began. 'We all belong to you and we will all return to you.'

Then she remembered words from the Koran.

'You merge night into daylight,
and daylight into night.
You draw the living from the dead,
and draw the dead from the living.
You provide for anyone You will
without any reckoning.'

Squatting there, in the dirt and the dust and the dark, she wept, and her tears spilt on to Aisha's face. Fatimah didn't wipe them away.

'They will wash you properly when you get home,' she whispered. 'But my tears are the first washing.'

She crawled back to the safe place under the arch and got a bottle of water from her school bag. She dragged out her mobile phone, too, but it was smashed up and didn't work. She flung it down in frustration. Then she crawled back again and, taking the corner of Aisha's hijab, she moistened it and very gently washed Aisha's mouth and closed her eyes.

☾ ☾ ☾

Fatimah's mind was numb; so was her body. She stayed there, crouched beside Aisha, too overwhelmed by grief to be frightened, unable to think or act any more. It took a while for her to realise that the sound she had heard before – the sound she had thought was Aisha – was still there. A faint moaning.

At last, it dawned on her. There was someone else here. Someone alive.

She listened again. The sound was very faint now.

Taking the precious bottle of water, she crawled away from Aisha's body. She stopped and listened again. The moaning was coming from a heap of fallen masonry close to a window. There were fragments of brightly-coloured glass everywhere, but it was lighter over here and the dust was beginning to settle. On the far side of the heap, she could just make out an inert form.

She was scared of what she'd find, but tried to stay calm as she crept forward, moving as smoothly as possible so as not to dislodge anything.

She recognised him. It was a boy from school. He was in the year above her, and she'd never spoken to him. She didn't even know his name. His eyes were shut and he looked in a bad way.

She leant over him. 'Can you hear me?' she asked.

He didn't answer.

Fatimah tried to think clearly. She could see that one of his legs was bent at an unnatural angle. There was a gash on his head and another on his arm.

She swallowed. She must do what she could for this boy.

His face was covered with dust, grime and blood. Fatimah took off her hijab and poured a little water on to it, then wiped his face. For a moment she worried about being unveiled, but then she dismissed the thought. What did it matter now?

The boy moaned again, but didn't open his eyes.

She sat back on her heels. She must try and do something about that leg. It looked awful and there was blood pouring from it. If he lost too much blood he would die. It was as simple as that.

There was already a large gash in the material of the trousers. Biting her lips, Fatimah tore the fabric further, until she could see the injury.

Momentarily she gagged and her hand flew to her mouth. His shin bone was shattered and was poking through the skin of his leg. He must be in agony.

Stop the blood flow. Raise the leg. From somewhere the words came into her head.

Praying that she was doing the right thing, she tried to thread her hijab under the boy's leg. She was unprepared for the scream of pain. She bent over his face. 'I'm sorry. I'm so sorry.'

His eyes were open and he stared up at her, uncomprehending.

'I'm trying to fix your leg,' she said. 'If I don't do something, it'll get much worse.'

The boy continued to stare at her.

'What's your name?' she asked.

His mouth moved, but she couldn't hear.

'Say it again,' she said. And she put her ear near to his mouth.

'Steve,' he whispered.

She stayed there, crouching beside him. 'Here, Steve,' she said, holding the bottle of water to his lips, 'try and have a little water.'

Obediently, Steve opened his lips and took a couple of sips.

'Steve, I'm going to try and tie up your leg to stop it bleeding,' she said.

He looked at her again. 'OK.'

'It's going to hurt,' she said. 'But it will be more comfortable when it's done.'

She didn't really believe this, but she had to do something if the leg was to be saved – if his life was to be saved. She wished she had something to give him to take the pain away.

This time she ignored the screams, avoided his thrashing arms, as she wound her scarf round the open wound and tied it as tightly as she could, to act as a tourniquet.

Suddenly his screams stopped. He had fainted.

She scrabbled around on the ground and pushed some fallen bricks towards him. Then she heaved the injured leg until it was resting on the pile of bricks, above the rest of his body. She watched anxiously, willing the bleeding to slow down.

The gush of blood slowed to a trickle, staining her hijab. Then, gradually, it stopped.

'Allah be praised,' she muttered. She undid the water bottle again and put some more water on his face.

'Wake up for me, Steve. You must stay awake.'

There was no response. Fatimah felt his pulse. It was very weak.

Gently, she slapped his face. 'Come back, Steve. You must stay awake.'

Slowly he opened his eyes again and groaned.

'Am I dead?'

For the first time since the blast, Fatimah smiled.

'No, you're not dead, Steve, and I'm going to make sure you stay that way.'

'Are you an angel or something?'

'Not an angel. Just a scared girl.'

'What's your name?'

'Fatimah.'

'Fa ... ti ... mah.'

He was drifting into unconsciousness again.

Fatimah started to pray. She prayed the second prayer of the day and asked forgiveness that she did so amongst all the dirt and dust and without washing. She thought of cleaning her hands and face with the remaining water, but decided she should keep it for Steve.

She quoted from the Koran. She asked for Allah's blessing on this non-Muslim boy.

'What are you doing?' asked Steve. His voice was slurred now.

'I'm praying,' said Fatimah.

'For me?'

She nodded. 'Yes.'

'I've never seen anyone pray before,' said Steve.

Then he started to mutter incoherently, moving his head from one side to the other.

For the first time, Fatimah started to wonder what might be happening outside. Surely the emergency services would be here by now? Surely they'd be rescued soon?

But it was a long time before she heard any sound except for the eerie creaking and shifting inside the church. Then, very faintly, there was the sound of a dog barking.

'Steve! They're sending sniffer dogs in! They'll find us soon.'

She shouted, as loudly as she could. 'We're here. Over here!'

She looked down at Steve. His eyes were shut. She must keep him talking. She slapped his face again.

'Wake up, Steve. You must keep awake!'

She started talking to him then. She told him about Aisha. She told him about Zahrah, about her mother and father and Hassan. She told him about how she wanted to be a doctor, about Uncle Ismail's pilgrimage – anything that came into her head, just to keep him awake.

She had no idea whether he was taking it in but his eyes were open now and he was thrashing about from side to side. At least he was conscious.

She shouted again, but her throat was parched and her voice cracked.

Then, faintly, she heard voices. She couldn't hear any words. But there were shouts. And then silence.

Summoning all her energy, she yelled out again. 'Here! Over here!' Then, even more urgently, as she looked down at Steve's ashen face, 'Please come quickly.'

The voices stopped, and she wondered if they'd given up. Perhaps they hadn't heard her. Surely they wouldn't give up, would they? Perhaps they'd gone to another part of the building.

Then she heard the sound of an engine. Perhaps

they had brought in a digger to clear the rubble outside. She could hear it more clearly now – coming forward with a rumble, then the noise of digging and scraping, then retreating.

Fearfully, she looked up. Directly above them, there was a huge crossbeam lodged precariously across two half-collapsed stone columns. As she heard the digger rumble towards the building again, she saw the beam trembling. It was very close to the edge of one of the pillars and it could fall at any moment.

She knelt over Steve and held his head in her hands to still it.

'Steve,' she said, as confidently as she could. 'I'm going to have to move you.'

He didn't seem to understand, so she said it again.

'It's going to hurt, Steve,' she said, choking back her tears. 'But if we don't move, that beam up there may fall on us.'

He must have understood her because, very briefly, he looked up at the beam.

'OK?' she said.

'OK,' he replied.

She put her hands under his arms and started to heave.

There was a piercing scream. But Fatimah didn't stop. He was heavy and he was inert. But somehow, with strength born out of desperation, she managed to drag him a little way over the rubble. It must be agony for him, she thought, but she kept her eyes fixed on the beam above. If she could get him back to the archway, they'd be safer.

She hauled again, closing her ears to his screams. They passed Aisha's body, but Fatimah didn't stop. She knew that if she looked at Aisha she would break down completely.

Then, at last, they were there. She sat behind Steve and cradled his head in her lap. He had stopped screaming and was moaning quietly. His eyes were shut. Fatimah put her hands over his and squeezed them.

'Hang in there, Steve.'

The noise from outside was louder now and she could feel the vibrations from the machine. Suddenly there was a deafening crash. Instinctively, Fatimah leant over Steve, trying to protect them both. She kept her eyes closed and she could sense the dust swirling about her, but nothing hit them; they were unharmed.

At last, she dared to look up. The huge crossbeam had crashed to the ground.

She was conscious of voices coming closer. They were calling her name – and Aisha's.

But she no longer had the strength to shout.

Every time she lifted her head, she saw Aisha's body and choked back the sobs.

Then there was a confusion of people inside the building. Paramedics, firemen, rescue workers, all coming towards her.

A man knelt down beside her.

'All right, love, we're here now.'

Fatimah didn't move. Steve's head was still in her lap and her hands held his. Her dark hair was covered in dust and her face was streaked with dirt.

Suddenly there was a flash and someone shouted. 'Who the hell let the Press in! Get them out of here!'

CHAPTER FOUR

Now there were more people – paramedics, firemen and a woman wearing a yellow jacket with 'DOCTOR' written across the back. A paramedic checked Fatimah over, looking in her eyes, feeling the lump on her head and inspecting her bruised arms and legs. Meanwhile, the doctor was with Steve. She gave him an injection and then talked quietly to the paramedics. They brought a stretcher and, very gently, started to lift Steve on to it.

Although his eyes were closed, he was conscious and the moment they began to move him, he started to scream with pain. But the team went on with their work, setting up a drip before they carried him away, trying to make his journey as smooth as possible while they climbed over the jagged heaps of rubble.

Fatimah bit her lip. She could still hear Steve's screams as the rescuers inched along the path cleared by the digger and carried him towards the entrance;

every one of his screams jarred through her and she found herself clutching the arm of the nearest paramedic.

'Will he be all right?' she asked.

'He'll go straight to the hospital, love. That's the best place for him.'

Fatimah relaxed a fraction; Steve was in good hands and there was nothing more she could do except to ask Allah to watch over him.

She was about to say a quick prayer when she suddenly realised that no one had said anything about Aisha. She turned around, looking towards the place where Aisha lay.

'My friend,' she said. 'My friend Aisha. She's over there.'

The paramedic gently smoothed the matted hair away from Fatimah's face.

'Yes, we've seen her,' he said quietly. 'We'll get her out just as soon as we've got you to hospital.'

'I couldn't save her.'

'No one could have saved her, love. But you did a great job with that lad. If you hadn't elevated his leg, he might be dead by now.'

Fatimah said nothing.

The man put his hands under her arms. 'Can you stand up?'

Fatimah slowly struggled to her feet. She swayed,

and the dust and the rubble all round her became blurred. From a long way away, she heard someone say, 'Get another stretcher. She's fainting.' Then nothing.

Nothing until she opened her eyes again. She was in the road outside, lying on a stretcher. Her mother was beside her, holding her hand, tears running down her face.

'I'm all right, Mum,' she said.

She tried to sit up, but her mother stopped her.

'Wait until you get to the hospital, Fatimah. Don't move.'

Her hands shaking, Fatimah's mother drew out her mobile and punched in a number. 'I must tell your father you're safe,' she muttered.

Fatimah struggled to a sitting position. She pushed away her mother's hand.

'Where is Auntie Leila?' she said, looking for Aisha's mother in the crowd of faces peering down at her.

There was an uneasy silence.

'Where is she?' She looked round anxiously.

Then, at the edge of the crowd, she saw her – Aisha's mother – Auntie Leila – and their eyes met.

'I tried to save her, Auntie,' said Fatimah. 'I tried to save Aisha, but she was dead when I got to her. I'm so sorry.'

But Auntie Leila couldn't hear. She just stared at Fatimah.

'Hush,' said Fatimah's mother. 'We know you did everything you could. Aisha's family will understand. Auntie Leila will understand.'

There were cameras flashing and a lot of noise. The police had cordoned off the road and were stopping the crowds getting too close but people were shouting out questions.

'How many were in the church?'

'Is anyone dead?'

Then a louder voice spoke, above the rest, a policeman with a loud hailer. 'Please keep away. The building is unsafe. Stand behind the cordon. Let the emergency services do their job.'

Fatimah was lifted into an ambulance. Her mother climbed in after her and the doors clanged shut behind them.

And at last there was peace until they reached the hospital.

There were more reporters and photographers around the entrance to the hospital, but the police and the paramedics kept them at bay and soon Fatimah was lying in a cubicle, waiting to be checked over again.

In the quiet of the hospital, away from the noise and confusion of the rescue, she felt shy and vulnerable. And for the first time since the accident, she realised that she was not wearing her hijab. Instinctively she put her hand to her head, worried that she was uncovered in front of strangers.

When the doctor came in, it was a young man. Fatimah's mother gently protested, 'Please, can you find a woman doctor? Please.'

The young man looked surprised, but he backed out and disappeared. A few minutes later, the woman doctor who had been at the church came into the cubicle. She was still wearing her yellow jacket and she had obviously just arrived. Her face and hands were clean but her hair still had dust in it. She smiled, and as she was taking Fatimah's temperature and feeling her bumps and bruises, she talked quietly to her.

'You were really brave, Fatimah. If you'd not been there, that boy would have certainly died. You saved his life.'

'How is Steve?' asked Fatimah.

'He's in the operating theatre right now,' said the doctor. 'His leg's pretty bad and they're trying to fix it.'

'Will he be all right?'

The doctor took her hand. 'Thanks to you, I'm sure he'll pull through, but he has some nasty injuries.'

Fatimah nodded. 'I'm glad he's going to be OK.'

Her mother was speaking. 'When can my daughter come home?' she asked.

'I think we should keep her here overnight. She's had a bump on the head and she's shocked. I'd like to keep an eye on her for another twenty-four hours. I'll get someone to take her up to the ward very soon.'

Then the doctor left, shrugging off her yellow jacket as she walked away.

Fatimah thought back to the moment when the accident happened. What exactly had happened? Nobody had said anything; the rescuers had been too busy getting them out and then, in the ambulance, she hadn't thought to ask.

'What caused the explosion, Mum?'

Her mother sighed and stroked Fatimah's arm. 'They are saying it was a bomb,' she said quietly.

Fatimah's eyes widened and they stared silently at each other. A bomb set off to destroy a Christian church. They both knew what that meant.

'They'll say it was Muslim extremists,' said Fatimah, flatly.

Her mother nodded. 'And they'll say it even though a Muslim girl was killed.'

For a few moments their thoughts were much the same. There would be more hostility, more taunts, more suspicion.

A nurse came into the cubicle.

'Your father and brother are here, Fatimah. Would you like to see them?'

Fatimah sat up. 'Yes, yes, of course!'

'They're waiting outside in reception,' said the nurse. 'I'll bring them through.'

A few moments later, Fatimah's father and Hassan came in. Her father rushed to her side and held her in his arms.

'We've been so worried about you,' he said, and tears were running down his cheeks. Fatimah had never seen her father cry before.

'It's all right, Dad,' said Fatimah, feeling choked up herself. 'It's all right. I'll be fine. I'm just a bit bruised.'

Hassan came forward awkwardly. 'I'm so sorry, little sister,' he said.

'You must have been very frightened,' said her father.

'She was very brave,' said her mother, 'She saved that boy's life.'

Her father frowned momentarily. 'Yes,' he said slowly. 'They told me.' Then, 'Did you know the boy, Fatimah?'

'No Dad. He is at our school but I'd never spoken to him. I didn't even know his name.'

She didn't tell him about the photographer who

had taken a picture the moment she and Steve had been found. She just prayed that it wouldn't be in the papers.

'And Aisha,' he was saying. 'We heard about Aisha.'

'I went to her first,' said Fatimah. 'But I couldn't help her, Dad. She was dead. Her neck was broken … she …' She couldn't finish the sentence.

'Merciful Allah,' whispered her father. 'What you have seen! What you have been through, my little daughter.'

'I remembered some of the prayers for the dead,' said Fatimah, wiping her eyes. 'I said as much as I could for her. And I washed her face.'

'You're a good girl,' he said, squeezing her hand, his eyes still brimming with tears. 'Such a good girl.'

The nurse came into the cubicle again. 'The porters will take you up to the ward now, Fatimah,' and she indicated a couple of young men standing outside, ready with a bed on wheels.

Fatimah's father looked across at the two men and opened his mouth to speak, then thought better of it. He withdrew his hand from Fatimah's and turned to the others. 'Come,' he said, 'I think we should leave her to rest now.'

Her mother had been expecting to go up to the ward with Fatimah. 'But …' she began.

'Come now,' he said gently.

Obediently, her mother kissed Fatimah goodbye and got up.

'We'll see you in the morning,' said her father. 'Then I hope we can take you home.'

Fatimah nodded and her eyes followed her family as they walked away down the corridor.

☾ ☾ ☾

He was with two others now – one man of his own age and one older – and they were speaking together quietly. 'You did a good job,' said the older man. 'Look at the filth around you. This is a sick society and Islam is the only cure. Our faith is a beautiful thing and we cannot have it polluted. Christianity is a cancer, Judaism is a cancer, materialism is a cancer, all destroying us.'

'But a Muslim girl was killed in the explosion,' said one of the young men.

'Then she is a martyr,' said the older man, 'and she is already in Paradise. Be strong. Think of our aims. Think of the greater good.'

'Allah be praised,' said the young men together.

☾ ☾ ☾

Steve was moaning and moving his head from side to side. He was confused. Someone was beside him, calling his name.

'Steve. Wake up, Steve. Can you open your eyes for me?'

Obediently, Steve forced his eyes open. For a few seconds, the recovery room swam into focus before he shut them again.

'Come on, Steve. Wake up.'

This time, when he opened his eyes, he saw that there was a nurse beside him, but he was too befuddled with drugs to know where he was.

'All right, Steve, you can go to sleep again now.'

Thankfully, he drifted back into unconsciousness.

When he woke again, he was more aware of what was going on. His leg was in traction, plastered up and suspended in a sort of sling, and one of his arms was strapped across his chest. His head ached badly and every time he took a breath, it felt as though his chest would explode.

'Where am I?' he said at last. 'What happened?'

A nurse was at his side. 'You were in an accident.'

Steve frowned. Through the waves of pain swam a vision of dust and rubble, of being lifted on to a stretcher – and of a dark-haired girl. He blinked and tried to remember, but he couldn't get a grip on it.

Then he saw his parents beside the bed, his mum

shocked and tearful, his dad unusually quiet.

His mum leant over and kissed him, then sat down by the bed and held his uninjured hand.

'Thank God you're alive,' she murmured, when at last she could speak. 'When we heard about the bomb, we phoned the school and they said you hadn't arrived. And we kept phoning and there was still no sign of you …'

'All right, love,' said his dad, gruffly. 'Don't upset him.'

Steve looked at them. He was still groggy and his thoughts were confused. What was Mum saying about a bomb?

'What happened?'

'They bombed St Luke's church,' said his mother.

'What? Who bombed it?'

'Muslim extremists, of course,' said his father. 'Who else?'

'We don't know that, Ben,' said Mum sharply.

'Who else would target a church, I'd like to know?'

Steve groaned, another wave of pain going through him.

'Are you in a lot of pain?' asked his mum. She looked up at the nurse. 'Can you give him anything?'

The nurse checked the chart at the end of Steve's bed. 'I'll give him an injection,' she said, and went away. She came back with a syringe in a dish.

'This will make you feel more comfortable, Steve, but it will make you sleepy, too.'

'Can we stay?' asked his mum.

'Yes, of course.'

As the drug began to take effect, Steve's face relaxed and he drifted in and out of sleep. His parents sat silently by his bed and the afternoon dragged into evening before Steve woke up properly again.

When he opened his eyes, he said, 'There was a girl. A dark-haired girl. She looked after me.'

His dad had nodded off to sleep, his chin sunk on his chest, but his mum was wide awake.

'We heard that there were two others in the church,' she said. 'Two girls.'

'What happened to them?'

'One died,' said his mum, 'but the other wasn't badly hurt.'

'She helped me,' said Steve, frowning and trying to remember. 'She tied up my leg.'

His mum nodded. 'The doctor told us. They said she probably saved your life.'

'I'd like to to see her,' said Steve, plucking at the sheets with his fingers. 'You know, to say thanks.'

Mum put her hand over his. 'She's here in hospital, too. I sent a message to her to say thank-you.'

'Oh. OK. But I'd still like to see her.'

'When you're a bit better, love.' She looked over at Steve's dad. He was snoring gently, slumped even further down the chair beside the bed. Steve tried to smile, but smiling hurt.

'I'd better get your dad home,' said his mum.

She shook him awake. 'Come on, Ben. We'll leave Steve to get some rest.' Steve's dad gradually surfaced and struggled to his feet. He stretched and yawned. 'We'll see you in the morning, son.'

When they'd gone, Steve tried to remember what had happened that morning. He remembered missing the bus, but after that, all he could see in his mind's eye was dust and rubble and people helping him, lifting him, and an agonising ride in an ambulance.

And the girl with dark hair.

☾ ☾ ☾

As Steve's parents left the hospital, a crowd of reporters surged towards them. Someone thrust a microphone in front of them.

'How's Steve? Is he going to be all right?'

Somehow, Steve's mum gathered her wits. 'He's been badly injured, but he's conscious now and he's in good hands. We're very grateful to everyone at the hospital.'

'Who do you think planted the bomb?'

This question was directed at them both, but Steve's father answered first. 'Muslim extremists,' he said at once, ignoring his wife's frantic look. 'Bloody Muslim fanatics.'

The reporter went on smoothly. 'And a girl saved your son's life, didn't she?'

Steve's mum broke in quickly. 'I believe so. We are so grateful to her. We hope to be able to see her soon and tell her in person.'

'And did you know,' continued the reporter, looking straight at Steve's father, 'that this girl – Fatimah – is a Muslim? And that it was her friend, another Muslim girl, who was killed in the explosion?'

Ben looked shocked. 'No, no, I didn't know,' he said, looking helplessly at Jackie as he realised what he'd just said. 'I'm sorry ... I didn't mean all Muslims are extremists ... I – '

'Thank you, sir,' said the reporter, melting away into the crowd.

☾ ☾ ☾

That evening, in the hospital ward, Fatimah anxiously watched the television news. The bombing of St Luke's had made the national headlines. Horrified, she saw pictures of the devastated church, of the rescuers going in, and of Steve and herself being brought out on stretchers.

Then she saw the clip when Steve's dad said he thought Muslim extremists were responsible for the bombing. The bit where he had tried to modify his remarks had been cut out.

Fatimah groaned, and one of the nurses heard her.

'Are you all right, love?'

She nodded, still staring at the screen. The nurse smiled. 'You've certainly hit the headlines. You're all over the evening paper, too.'

Fatimah stared at her. 'Have you got a copy of the paper?' she asked.

'There's one in the staff room. I'll bring it in later.'

Fatimah waited in a frenzy of worry. Would there be a photo of her holding Steve? And, if there was, how would it look to her friends, the people at the mosque, other Muslim families?

Surely they'd realise that she had to help another human being? Surely no one – not even the strictest of her relations – would condemn her for that? Would they?

At last, the nurse came in, smiling and tossed a copy of the newspaper into Fatimah's lap.

Dry-mouthed, Fatimah picked up the newspaper

and stared at the photo on the front page.

There she was, her hair loose, cradling Steve's head in her lap, her hands entwined in his. And underneath the photo, the caption screamed:

IS THIS LOVE ACROSS THE DIVIDE?
MUSLIM GIRL SAVES SCHOOLBOY FRIEND

It went on to give her details and Steve's details and as an afterthought, mentioned that her friend Aisha had died in the blast.

Fatimah read and re-read the article. The implication was horribly clear; she had saved her white boyfriend and left her Muslim girlfriend to die. That is how people would see it. That is how people in the Muslim community would interpret it. Some of them, at least.

Her head throbbed. She let the newspaper slide off the bed, lay back and closed her eyes.

CHAPTER FIVE

Fatimah slept badly. The shock of all that had happened was beginning to kick in. She felt sick and she couldn't stop shaking. All through the evening, people had come to check her out: a doctor, a counsellor and, briefly, two policemen and a policewoman. The police were very gentle with her and as soon as she started to get upset, they went away.

Wearily, she made her way to the bathroom to wash and, briefly, to pray, but she found it impossible to concentrate. Her brain was sluggish and her limbs felt heavy. She came back to her hospital bed tense and frustrated. And when she settled down and tried to sleep, the events of the day crowded in. She saw again the inside of the church, the rubble and the dust. And always there was Aisha. Sometimes Aisha was chatting to her, laughing and joking. And sometimes Aisha lay still with her neck flopping over. Fatimah saw Steve in her dreams, too, with blood pouring from his leg, writhing in agony.

She thought about the present she had bought for Aisha for Eid – that special scarf she had seen in town. Aisha would never wear it now.

Several times in the night Fatimah woke, shouting, and the night nurse came over, offering to give her something to make her sleep. Fatimah refused at first, but at last she gave in and took a sleeping pill. After that there were no more dreams.

She was woken early from her drugged sleep by the sounds of hospital life, the clang of trolleys, the chatter of the nurses as they changed shifts.

A woman came round selling the morning papers. Fatimah had no money on her, but she didn't want to read them anyway. She knew the bombing would be a prominent feature in them. But she couldn't fail to see one of the headlines: *Muslim extremists strike again.*

A nurse she'd not seen before came and sat on the edge of her bed.

'How are you feeling, love?' she asked.

She wished people would stop asking that. How does she think I feel? she thought. I've lost my best friend and my faith is being rubbished.

'A bit shaky,' she replied.

'Of course you are. You're bound to be, after what you've been through.' The nurse plumped up her pillows. 'Breakfast in a minute,' she said cheerfully, as she walked briskly away.

As soon as the nurse left, Fatimah heaved herself out of bed. Her legs were like jelly. She felt worse than she had felt yesterday. The doctor had warned her this might happen. Delayed shock, she had called it. Slowly, she forced herself along the corridor to do her washing. Again, she had to make her praying brief and it bothered her that, in her dopey state, she couldn't even work out the direction of Mecca.

After breakfast, she asked one of the nurses when she could go home.

'Oh, I can't tell you, love,' she replied. 'Wait till the doctor's been round.'

'Well,' said Fatimah shyly, 'Can you tell me if there's a place where I can pray?'

The nurse looked blank for a moment. Then: 'Oh yes, sure,' she said. 'There's a Muslim prayer room on the ground floor, I think.'

'Can I go there?'

The nurse looked uncertain. 'Better wait till the doctor's been,' she repeated.

After she'd eaten, Fatimah felt a bit stronger. She lay back against the pillows and closed her eyes.

A nurse told her that her mother was on the phone at the nurses' desk and Fatimah took the call.

'How did you sleep, darling? How are you feeling?

When will they let you come home?'

'I'm OK, Mum. Bit shaky. I don't know when they'll let me home. I'll know more when the doctor's been to see me.'

'All right, I'll phone a bit later. Have you got your mobile with you? Can you use it there?'

Fatimah swallowed. 'No, Mum,' she said. 'I lost it in the church.'

'Yes. Yes, of course. Stupid of me.'

Fatimah walked slowly back to her room. They had put her in a room by herself and, as she glanced down the ward ahead, she was aware of the curious glances. Bad news travelled fast, it seemed. Everyone knew who she was.

She felt lonely, so she left the door open and stood by her bed, watching as people passed by in the corridor.

She saw the police before the nursing staff saw them, and she knew immediately that they had come to speak to her again. Her stomach clenched as they approached her, with a nurse in tow.

'We won't keep you long, Fatimah,' said the policewoman. 'We'd just like to ask you a few more questions.'

Fatimah nodded and sat down heavily on the edge of her bed.

The nurse hovered in the doorway. 'Ten minutes,'

she said. 'She's been through a lot, you know.'

The policewoman smiled. 'OK,' she said.

They were gentle with her but asked probing questions. Was there anyone she knew – any young man in her community – who had been abroad recently? Who might have been influenced by radicals? Had she known Steve before the bombing? Had she seen any suspicious package, any suspicious people?

To each question, Fatimah shook her head. She could tell them nothing.

Then the trembling started again and the policewoman put an arm round her.

'You're being very brave, Fatimah, and we won't keep you much longer,' she said. 'But we need to catch the terrorist who planted the bomb; and we need to know who was behind it.'

Fatimah frowned, hardly able to take in what she said.

'A terrorist?'

The policewoman nodded. 'Yes, it looks as though it was the work of an Islamic terrorist, I'm afraid.'

Fatimah's anger welled up again. 'How do you know? How do you know that the person was a Muslim? Not all terrorists are Muslims!'

The policeman cleared his throat. 'Of course they're not,' he said gently. 'But I'm afraid, on this occasion, there's not much doubt.'

'How? How can you be so certain?'

'We have a good forensic team,' said the policewoman. 'We know how the bomb was made and how it was detonated.'

'So, do you have a suspect?'

The policeman shook his head. 'No,' he said slowly. 'But we know the organisation.'

Fatimah felt suddenly chilled.

'OK, Fatimah,' said the policeman, 'We'll leave it there for now, but we'll be back to see you at home.' He put his notebook back in his top pocket. 'And if there's anything you want to tell us, please get in touch right away.' He handed her a card. 'Call this number and it will reach me wherever I am.

Just as they were leaving, Fatimah said. 'Have you seen Steve? The boy who was hurt? Is he OK?'

The policewoman shook her head. 'They don't want us to interview him just yet,' she said.

'Is he very bad?'

'Apparently he's out of danger,' said the policewoman, 'but he's in a lot of pain.' Then she added, 'We hope to be able to speak to him soon.'

When they had gone, Fatimah sighed. She hated all this waiting. How much longer would she be kept here?

At last the doctor showed up. A man, this time, but

Fatimah said nothing. If she asked to be examined by a woman doctor, that would mean more waiting.

He was a young Indian or Pakistani. Fatimah wondered if he, too, was a Muslim. He examined her quickly and professionally, looking into her eyes with a torch, making her follow his finger with her eyes and asking about headaches and lack of balance. When he'd finished, she said, 'Can I go home today?'

He smiled. 'Yes, I don't see why not, but if you have any symptoms, you must let us know. Any bad headaches, double vision, dizziness ...'

Fatimah nodded impatiently. 'Yes, yes, of course.'

Then, just as he was leaving, she said, 'How is Steve? Do you know?'

'The boy who was with you?'

Fatimah nodded.

'Well, I've just been to see him. He's feeling very sore, but he's out of danger. But he'll have to stay in hospital for a while.'

'Can I visit him?'

The doctor hesitated for a moment – and in that moment, Fatimah sensed why. He's a Muslim, too, she thought. He doesn't think I should. Then he continued. 'Well, yes, I suppose so,' and he turned on his heel and walked out of the door.

Fatimah felt suddenly defiant. Why shouldn't she go and see Steve? OK, perhaps her parents and her brother might not like her to be in the same room with him. No young girl should be left alone with a man unless that man is a relative. But hadn't she already been alone with him? Alone in the church for all that time, with only poor Aisha's broken body for company?

Only twenty-four hours ago, she thought grimly, she would never even have considered going against her parents' wishes. But the bomb had changed everything. Her secure life had been turned on its head. Yesterday morning, bomb outrages had been things which went on in other cities, committed by mad extremists. Her family were peace-loving. They were British and proud of it; they didn't want to undermine their own way of life. And now here it was, on their doorstep. Hatred, raw hatred, bubbling up to the surface. Hatred and fear.

Shakily, she got out of bed, put on the hospital dressing-gown and slippers and went down the corridor to the nurses' station. She phoned home.

Her father answered, his voice strained.

'Dad! What are you doing at home? Why aren't you at work?'

'I couldn't go to work today,' he said. 'I've just come back from the mosque.'

Fatimah was taken aback. Her father never missed a day's work.

'Dad, I can come home now,' she said.

'That's wonderful news,' he said. Then, 'Here's your mother.'

'We'll come right away. We'll come and fetch you straight away,' said her mother.

'No rush, Mum. I've got to sign forms and things. Could you bring me some clean clothes?'

'Of course. We'll be there soon.'

Fatimah replaced the phone. Then she went to the nurse on duty.

'Can you find out if I can see Steve?' she asked.

'Steve?'

'The boy who was hurt in yesterday's bombing.'

'Oh … oh yes, of course.'

'I want to say goodbye before I leave,' said Fatimah.

The nurse punched some numbers into the phone keypad and spoke to someone at the other end.

'He's out of Intensive Care,' she said. 'He's in a room on his own. Ward G8 on the next floor up. But check with the nurse before you visit him, dear. I've told her you're coming.'

Fatiman nodded. 'Yes, sure.'

She walked to the lift and pressed the 'up' button. Inside, she tightened the belt on the dressing-gown. It was quite a modest garment, she thought, smiling to herself. But she had no hijab; it was probably in a hospital waste bin by now. But then, her head had been uncovered yesterday, too, all that time in the church.

She got out of the lift, walked slowly to the locked double doors at the entrance to Ward G8 and spoke into the intercom. There was a buzz and she pushed the doors and went inside.

At the nurses' desk they told her to wait. Suddenly Fatimah was desperate to sit down, but there was no seat in sight, so she clung to the edge of the desk, her legs shaking with the effort of walking the short distance from lift to ward.

At last the nurse bustled back. 'He's awake,' she said, smiling, 'and he says he'd like to see you.' She pointed to a room off the main ward. 'He's in there.' Then, as Fatimah was walking away, 'Don't stay long, dear. He's very sore and tired.'

Fatimah walked up to the closed door. She took a deep breath and gave a tentative knock.

'Come in.'

She opened the door and went inside. Steve tried to raise his head as Fatimah came in, but the effort was too much for him and it lolled back on the pillows. But he did manage a crooked smile.

'Hi,' he said. 'Thanks for coming.'

Fatimah started to tremble. Seeing him again, so pale and vulnerable, brought yesterday's horrible events back with a vengeance and, unbidden, the sight of Aisha's body was there in her head. Her lovely, funny Aisha. Life would never be the same without her … Stop it, she told herself. Don't think like that. Concentrate.

She clasped her hands to stop them shaking and smiled back at Steve.

'How are you?'

Steve made a face.

'Not great.'

Fatimah nodded at his leg. 'Does it hurt a lot?'

'Mmm. But they've given me stuff to take the pain away.'

Fatimah stood awkwardly by the edge of the bed. 'The doctor said you'd have to stay here for a bit.'

Steve smiled again. 'Yeah. But, hey, what's a few more days in hospital? If it wasn't for you, I might be dead.'

Fatimah blushed. 'I hope I helped.'

Instinctively, Steve put his hand out and touched her arm. It was a natural gesture that he would have made to any of his mates, male or female – though, if he'd been stronger, it would have been a light punch.

Fatimah didn't move, but her blush deepened.

'Of course you helped, Fatimah. I don't remember much about it, to be honest, just your face above me and you talking all the time. But they told me how you dragged me free and how you bound up my leg. They said I would have bled to death or been crushed by that beam if you hadn't been there.'

'I did what I could... I want to be a doctor one day, if I can pass all the exams.' She stopped, embarrassed. Why am I telling him this? she thought.

There was an awkward silence. Fatimah drew up a chair and sat down.

'Steve.'

'Mmm.'

'Have you seen the papers?'

'No. 'Fraid not. Not really up to reading yet.'

There are pictures of us all over them,' she said.

'Really! How cool is that?'

Suddenly Fatimah felt angry with him. He might be badly hurt and in pain, but she couldn't suppress her exasperation.

'It isn't cool. It's terrible!'

'What d'you mean? Why?'

'You just don't get it, do you?'

Steve was frowning. 'Look, you'll have to explain, Fatimah. My brain's not working too well just now.'

Fatimah bit her lip. 'I'm sorry. I know you're feeling really bad, but you've got to understand, Steve.' She hesitated. 'They've plastered photos of us all over the place,' she began, stuttering slightly with embarrassment. 'When the emergency people got to us, someone from the Press was there, too. They took this photo of me... of me with your head in my lap, holding your hands.'

'But ... you were helping me,' said Steve, looking puzzled.

'Exactly. And that's all I was doing. You know that and I know that. But ... but Steve, you should see what they are saying in the papers.'

'What? Are they saying we're an item?'

Fatimah nodded miserably and suddenly she felt tears welling up. 'They're saying that and they're saying I saved you instead of saving my friend Aisha.'

'But that's rubbish! My parents said the other girl had died instantly.'

'I know it's rubbish. But you have no idea how it looks to other Muslims.' She sniffed and rubbed her eyes. 'I come from a strict family, Steve. Our religion is very important to us. If any ... any of my friends or relations think that I was your ...' She couldn't bring herself to say the word.

'My girlfriend?'

Fatimah swallowed. 'Yes. If they think that, it could cause trouble.'

'What sort of trouble?'

Fatimah sighed. 'If ... if anyone thinks that I've ... I've been out with a non-Muslim boy ... well, it could make things very difficult for me – and for my family.

People talk. Even though there's no truth in it, a rumour will start. The newspapers might get hold of it. And it could cause trouble for you, too. And for your family.'

Suddenly Steve groaned and Fatimah saw the pain in his face. Poor boy, she thought, he's not taking this in at all.

'Oh, I'm sorry, Steve. I shouldn't be saying all this now. You're sick and you're hurting. I'll go. But I just wanted to warn you.'

Steve put his hand out and touched her arm again. 'Please don't go,' he said.

'I must. My parents are coming to fetch me.'

'Will you come and see me again?'

Fatimah got up. 'I'll try,' she said.

Then, as she reached the door of his room, she hesitated. 'Just be careful, Steve. Be really careful what you say.'

'OK,' he said.

But, as she walked away, back towards the security doors, she knew that he didn't really understand. How could he?

She passed the nurses' station and saw the policeman and woman there, talking to the same nurse who had shown her the way to Steve's room. Quickly Fatimah turned away. She didn't want to be seen coming out of Steve's room.

Wearily she made her way back to her hospital bed. There was a buzz of conversation in the ward which stopped abruptly as she came into sight. She shrugged. She must expect the rest of the patients to whisper about her. After all, they had seen the papers.

She stood at the window looking out over the rooftops of the town. The sky was still grey and the trees in the hospital grounds were heavy with drenched foliage. So often, on days like this, her grandmother talked longingly of the dryness, the heat and sunshine of Pakistan. How strange England must have seemed to her when she first came here, thought Fatimah. Yet I can't imagine living anywhere else. This is my home. I'd love to see Pakistan one day but I don't belong there. I belong here.

She continued to stand there, unmoving, until her thoughts were interrupted by a knock at the door.

The nurse came in. 'Your parents are here, Fatimah,' she said.

Fatimah looked past the nurse – and there were her mother and father and Hassan waiting outside. At the sight of them, all her pent-up emotions bubbled over and she burst into tears. She ran forward into her mother's outstretched arms.

CHAPTER SIX

In clean clothes and a fresh hijab, Fatimah felt more in control as she left the hospital. Her mother held her arm tightly as they reached the exit.

'There will be people from the Press there, darling,' she said.

Fatimah nodded, but said nothing.

'Don't speak to them, Fatimah,' said her father. 'It is best to say nothing.'

'Yes, I understand.'

But she was unprepared for the huge number confronting her outside the hospital. As she and her family stepped out into the muggy grey day, a mass of journalists and photographers surged forward.

'How are you feeling, Fatimah?'

'Is Steve really your boyfriend?'

'What do you think about the people who planted the bomb?'

Fatimah was seething, but she said nothing. She

could feel her mother's grip tightening on her arm as they walked silently towards the car park, her father and Hassan leading the way, trying to forge a path through the mass of people. But the crowd closed behind them, cutting them off.

Suddenly, she and her mother were in the middle, unprotected.

Then a loud hailer boomed over the hubbub.

'Police. Clear a space for them. Come on, you've got your photos. Give the poor girl a chance.'

Fatimah was frightened. She knew none of these people wanted to hurt her. She knew they just wanted her story, but she was sweating with panic.

'Mum!' she shouted. 'Don't let them near me!'

Then the crowd moved away and at last there was a clear space for them to walk to the car park. Flanked by police, Fatimah and her mother joined up with her father and Hassan. But, once they were in the car, the crowd surged forward again, shouting at the closed windows, cameras flashing, running after the car as it gathered speed and drove away.

Fatimah clung to her mother in the back seat.

'Is this how it is going to be, Mum? Have I got to live with all this?'

Her mother held her close. 'Shhh, my darling. We'll soon be home.'

But there were more crowds outside their house

and they had to fight their way to the front door.

'Please,' said her father. 'Please leave us alone.'

'Just a few questions, then we'll go,' shouted a reporter.

Fatimah's father faced the cameras. 'I will answer any questions. Let my family go inside, please.'

Hassan pushed Fatimah and her mother towards the door. He dropped the key in his hurry to get them inside and they were almost flattened by the surge of the crowd while he picked it up and fumbled to get it into the lock. Then, at last, he got the door open and they fell inside, slamming the door behind them and leaving Fatimah's father to face the cameras on his own.

Again, the same questions – questions about Muslim extremists, to which Fatimah's father said, 'We have nothing in common with men of violence. We are peace-loving people.'

'What about your daughter's relationship with the young man she saved?'

Fatimah's father was trembling but he kept calm. 'My daughter saved a young man's life,' he said slowly. 'I am very proud of her.'

'Is Steve her boyfriend?'

'My daughter does not have boyfriends,' he replied. 'That is not our custom.'

He didn't trust himself to say more, so he

held up his hand. 'Forgive me,' he said. 'I must be with my family.'

Hassan opened the front door briefly and hauled his father inside. They looked at each other, bewildered and helpless, the strain showing on every face. Fatimah's mother went round the rooms on the ground floor and drew the curtains, shutting out the morning light and any prying eyes. She switched on the lights and then went to make some tea. Fatimah started to follow her into the kitchen, but her mother stopped her.

'Go and sit down, darling. I'll bring it in to you in a moment.'

Then, as she walked down the passage, she pointed to a heap of mail on the table. 'There are a lot of cards for you; people have been very kind. The phone hasn't stopped ringing and so many friends have come to see us.'

Listlessly, Fatimah started looking through the cards. Some from school friends, some from relations. The kind words made her cry. But the one that moved her most was from Aisha's mother and father. There was no trace of blame for Aisha's death – only concern for her and gratitude that she had been with her friend at the end.

None of these people believe the lies printed in the papers, she thought. Perhaps she was being stupid; perhaps everyone would understand after all. Perhaps everyone would realise that she could not have helped Aisha and that she had to help Steve. As a good Muslim, that was her duty and people would see that.

She sighed and let herself relax a little. Now that she had heard from Aisha's family, she must go and visit them. She sat looking at their card, the tears falling freely down her cheeks, then she kissed it briefly and set it down on the table with the others. For a moment her mood lifted. Perhaps there would be no backlash after all.

But her optimism didn't last long. She slit open another envelope and drew out a single sheet of paper. She frowned as she unfolded it. There was just one line of writing on lined paper torn from a pad. As she read the note, she started to tremble.

Biting her lip, she screwed up the paper in a ball and flung it away into the far corner of the room. Then she put her hands to her face. This was far worse than she had expected.

She could still see the words, slashed in heavy black felt tip across the page:

WHITE BOY'S WHORE

The words burned into her brain and she started to tremble again. Who was it? Who had sent that note? And how did they know where she lived?

She looked at the scrunched-up note in the corner, then picked it up between her finger and thumb and tucked it into her sleeve. Whatever happened, she mustn't let her family see it. The scratchy ball of paper lodged close to her skin, and her flesh rose in goose pimples of disgust.

She sat down again, pale and shaken, until her mother came in with the tea. Then she raised her tear-stained face and looked up. Her mother set down the tray and came up to her. She took Fatimah's hands between her own and gently rubbed them.

'You are so cold.'

For a moment, Fatimah thought of telling her mother about the note, but she couldn't bring herself to do it. She was so ashamed.

'Still a bit wobbly,' she said. 'I dunno… all these cards. People being kind…'

Her mother poured out a mug of sweet tea and noticed how Fatimah's hands trembled as she held it up to her lips.

'You are still shocked,' she said gently. 'You must give it time.'

The day dragged on and no one left the house; they felt like prisoners in their own home. The phone rang constantly, but when afternoon turned into evening, and it was time for prayers, they took it off the hook.

It was only when she was saying the familiar prayers, surrounded by her family, that Fatimah at last felt calmer. One nutter had sent her a vicious note. She must not let that upset her. Whoever it was must be mad. Any normal person would know she had done nothing wrong.

Later, Hassan whispered to his parents and made towards the front door.

'Where are you going?' asked Fatimah.

Hassan looked at his father, who nodded, 'I'm going to buy the evening paper,' he said.

'Don't bother,' muttered Fatimah. 'There'll just be more lies about me, I expect.'

Her father's face was strained. 'We need to know what is being said. If there are more lies, then we need to know what they are so we can deny them.' Fatimah shrugged and looked down at her feet.

When Hassan returned, he looked flustered.

'Everywhere I went, people stopped to talk,' he said.

'Did anyone insult you, say things about me?' asked Fatimah.

'No, of course not,' said Hassan, quickly. But he didn't meet her eyes when he replied. He's lying, she thought, but then she told herself to stop being so paranoid.

Her parents and Hassan quickly looked through the papers.

'It's not too bad,' said her mother. 'There's not so much about you: more about why the church was a target for the bomber.'

Fatimah looked up, suddenly taking an interest. 'And why was it?' she asked.

'Apparently the man in charge there – the vicar – has been talking with the imam from the mosque. There's been good dialogue between them, it says, and they are running inter-faith meetings, trying to build up trust between communities.'

Fatimah frowned. 'And that's why the church was a target? Because these men were talking to each other?'

Her father nodded. 'It looks like it,' he said slowly. 'There are people who want to keep us apart. We all know that.'

'You don't believe that, Dad, do you? You don't believe that people of different faiths shouldn't speak to one another, try to understand one another?'

Her father sighed, and Fatimah noticed that he was fiddling with his watch strap; he always did this when he was nervous or unsure.

'It's all so different now ...' he began.

Hassan broke in. 'I think it's good,' he said firmly. 'We must speak to one another. We must try to understand one another. Religious intolerance is just stupid.'

His father looked surprised. 'I didn't know you held such strong views, son.'

Hassan met his father's eyes. 'You're right, Dad, when you said it's different now.'

'Tell me how you think it is different, Hassan. I'm interested.'

Fatimah heard the warning signs in the pitch of her father's voice. He was not used to being challenged by his family.

Hassan cleared his throat. 'Well, your father and mother came here and all they wanted to do was to work hard and bring up their families. But they kept themselves apart and didn't expect to be accepted as British.'

Fatimah looked at Hassan in astonishment. She couldn't believe this was her brother speaking so frankly to their father.

'And you think that your mother and I are the same?' said his father.

'No, not exactly. It is easier for you because you have been born here and grew up here. But you still think of yourselves as different – special.'

'And you don't?'

'I'm British, Dad. So is Fatimah. I don't make excuses for who I am or hide my faith, but I have friends who challenge me at college, whose views I respect. And I challenge them, too. We discuss these things frankly. I don't avoid their questions. What I'm saying … ' – he hesitated, trying to find the right words – 'all I'm saying is, it's good to discuss these things … to learn about other points of view.'

There was an uneasy silence. Then his father spoke.

'One of those telephone calls was from the imam,' he said, changing the subject. 'He wants to visit us.'

'Of course,' muttered Hassan. 'Of course he must come.' But he turned away. He would never get his dad to admit that others held equally valid views on religion and codes of behaviour. As far as his father was concerned, there was only one true God, only one true way. No one else's God, no one else's way of life was right. And that was that.

☾ ☾ ☾

At the hospital, Steve's room was full of people. His mum and dad were there and three of Steve's friends from school. His mum looked anxiously at Steve's flushed face.

'Come on, Ben,' she said, tugging at his father's

sleeve. 'Let's leave him alone with his mates for a bit.'

Steve's father heaved himself up from the chair where he'd been sitting and unwillingly followed her out into the corridor.

'They shouldn't be here,' he said crossly. 'You heard what the nurse said.'

'Loosen up, love,' said Jackie. 'He can rest when they've gone, but you can see how they're cheering him up.'

Ben shrugged. 'OK. Let's grab a quick coffee.'

Tom and Mark, Steve's two best mates, were there, and Katie, a girl from the year below who was going out with Mark. They were chatting and joking with Steve about something that had happened at school that day.

'For God's sake,' pleaded Steve. 'Stop it. It really hurts when I laugh.' He held his hand to his aching ribs.

'Are you OK?' said Katie.

Steve pulled a face. 'Better than I was.'

'You really had us scared when we saw the pictures of you being brought out from that church,' she said, suddenly serious.

'Yeah,' said Tom. 'You looked so bad, we thought you might not make it.'

Steve rubbed his forehead. It felt hot and clammy. 'I wouldn't have made it – if it hadn't been for Fatimah,' he said quietly.

And again, her face was there in front of him, dark hair and big serious eyes, sitting with him, willing him to live.

'She's a nice girl – she's in my year,' said Katie.

Steve looked at her. 'Oh yeah? Do you know her, then?'

Katie shrugged. 'Not well. She's in some of my classes and she plays netball in our team. But she doesn't come out with us or anything. Well, they don't, do they? They all stick together.'

'What's she like?'

Katie screwed up her face. 'Umm. She's quite quiet; she's got some good Muslim friends in our year. She was really close to Aisha – the girl who died – and she's pretty clever, I think.'

Mark nudged Steve and he winced with pain. 'She's a looker. Pity she wears that scarf all the time, though.'

Suddenly Steve felt irritated. 'She covers her head because it's their custom, you idiot.'

Mark nodded to the others. 'Thought so,' he said, to the room in general. 'He fancies her.'

'I do not,' said Steve, raising himself on his elbow.

'Yes, you do!' said Mark. 'You're blushing! I guess the papers were right when they said you were Romeo.'

'Stop it!' said Steve, really angry now. 'The girl saved my life. It doesn't mean I fancy her.'

'OK, OK, calm down. I was just having a laugh.'

'Well don't. Not about her.'

'Hey,' said Katie, changing the subject quickly, 'Craig's really upset.' She turned to the others. 'You know, the one who wants to go out with that other Muslim girl, Zahrah.'

Steve was still trembling with fury. He couldn't bear any criticism of Fatimah. But he was curious.

'What's he upset about?' he asked.

'Well, since the bombing, Zahrah won't have anything to do with him – won't even speak to him, she's so scared.'

'Scared?'

'Yeah. Scared she'll get the same treatment Fatimah's getting. You know, talk in their families about a Muslim girl not keeping herself pure, being seen with a non-Muslim boy, that sort of stuff.'

Steve frowned. 'Is Fatimah being talked about at school, then?'

Katie shrugged. 'You know what it's like. There'll always be rumours.'

'Well,' said Steve angrily. 'You can tell anyone who wants to know that there's nothing between me and Fatimah. Nothing. I'd never even spoken to her before the bombing.'

Tom and Mark laughed. 'Don't get all stressed, Steve. We're only teasing you.'

Suddenly, Steve wanted to cry. He bit his lip and turned his face away from them.

Luckily, his parents came back just then.

'You'd better go now,' said his mum to his friends. 'Thanks ever so much for coming. It's really cheered him up. But he gets tired very easily.'

The three of them started to leave.

'See you, Steve. Hope you feel better soon.'

His mum went with them to the door. 'Come and see him again,' she said quietly. 'He'll need his friends. He's still very shocked but he's getting better all the time.'

Soon after this, Ben and Jackie left too, and Steve was alone. Fatimah's words echoed in his mind. 'Be very careful, Steve.'

He hadn't realised what it might mean for her, all that silly stuff in the papers: someone – some nutter out there – might actually believe it. Poor Fatimah.

And he hadn't been honest with his friends, either. He did like her. He liked her a lot. And not just because she had saved his life. She was unlike any girl he had ever known. And he did fancy her.

He shifted his position and tried to get more comfortable. Don't even go there, Steve, he thought to himself. That way is a dead end.

On their way home in the car, Jackie turned to Ben as they stopped at traffic lights.

'We must go and see that girl who saved Steve. We should thank her properly. Take her a present.'

Ben grunted.

Suddenly Jackie was really irritated with him. All her worry about Steve erupted in anger.

'Can't you put your prejudices aside for one moment and go and see the girl who saved your son's life?'

Ben didn't answer. Jackie sat there seething. 'Well if you won't come with me, I'll go on my own,' she said.

Ben cleared his throat. 'Couldn't we just ... write her a letter or something?' he said weakly.

'No we could not!' shouted Jackie. 'And I think it would do you good to open your eyes and see how some other people live.'

Ben was shocked. Jackie had never spoken to him like this.

'All right, love, all right. It's just that I would feel uncomfortable.'

'This isn't a comfortable situation,' she snapped. 'It's not comfortable for that poor girl – her best friend died in there – and it's not comfortable for Steve, either.'

They drove home in silence. There were still a few reporters hanging about the house but they managed to get inside without speaking to anyone.

The answerphone light was flashing, and Jackie played back a few messages. She listened to two of them, writing quickly on the notepad by the phone. But then, at the third one, she drew in a sharp breath and stepped back as if the phone was alive.

'What is it?' asked Ben.

Jackie turned to him, her eyes frightened. 'It's horrible,' she whispered.

Ben walked over to the phone and replayed the message.

It was a man's voice.

'Keep your boy away from Muslim girls or he'll be in bad trouble.'

Quickly, Ben punched in 1471. But the caller had withheld his number.

They looked at each other. Jackie shivered.

'We'd better get the police,' said Ben grimly. 'They'll be able to trace the call, I expect.'

Jackie took a deep breath. 'We'd better listen to the other two calls,' she said, 'just in case ... ' She put out her hand to him and he held it tight, then he pressed PLAY.

But the last two calls weren't threatening.

One was from a friend and the other was from the vicar of St Luke's church, asking if he could come and see them.

'What does he want with us?' said Ben, frowning. 'We're not churchgoers.'

Jackie shrugged. 'There's been a lot about him in the papers, how he's been trying to get Muslims and Christians together.'

'Huh,' said Ben. 'And look where it's got him!'

'Still,' said Jackie slowly, 'he sounds like a brave man. Maybe we should see him.'

'We don't want to be seen hobnobbing with the likes of him, Jackie. Use your head, girl. He's been stirring things up. And what happens? His church gets bombed! No, we should keep well out of it. We don't want to get involved.'

Jackie looked up sharply. 'Not get involved? Ben, we are involved. Your son nearly died.'

Ben didn't reply. He picked up the phone and called the police. 'I'd like to report a threatening phone call,' he said.

☪ ☪ ☪

The older man was really angry. He clutched the shoulder of the young man beside him.

'I know what you have been doing. Phone calls, notes.

How many times must I tell you? Keep a low profile. Go about as if nothing has happened.'

The young man looked up defiantly, his eyes ablaze. 'We must root out anything that pollutes Islam,' he said. 'They needed to be told. That disgusting photograph in the newspaper ...'

'You don't do it like that! Not operating on your own. You are part of a cell. You must not be identified and you must operate only when you get instructions.'

'But ...'

'No buts. Where is your humility?'

The young man stood up. 'I am ready to die for the cause.'

The older man nodded. 'Your time will come,' he said. 'No doubt your time will come.'

CHAPTER SEVEN

The week dragged on. Fatimah longed to go back to school, to see her friends, to get on with her life, but her parents and the doctor said she should wait a few more days. Her teachers came round with work for her and she tried to concentrate on her revision. Her GCSE exams would start soon; she must do well in them.

But she was restless. Before she could get down to her work, she wanted to see Aisha's family. Aisha's mum, Auntie Leila, had been like a second mother to her. And Aisha's brother Habib was good friends with Hassan. They had all grown up together.

'Please, Mum. Please let's go round to see Auntie Leila.'

Her mother looked at her father. He nodded.

'She's right. We must go and offer our condolences. It has been too long already. It's just that … are you sure you are strong enough, Fatimah?'

Fatimah nodded. 'I can't get down to my work, Dad. I can't concentrate. I want to see Auntie Leila and the rest of the family.'

So it was arranged, and the next evening, they all went to visit Aisha's family.

Fatimah's heart began to race as they approached the house. The last time she had been there was the day of the bombing. The last time that door had opened for her, Aisha had come rushing out, hijab skewed, full of high spirits, giggling and sweeping Fatimah off down the road.

She held tight to her mother's hand as they got closer.

'Are you all right?' whispered her mum. 'We can go back.'

Fatimah shook her head. 'We must go.'

Habib came to the door. Fatimah was shocked at the way he looked. His face was thin and tense and he looked years older. The carefree student had disappeared.

'Come in, please,' he said, holding the door open for them. Hassan clasped Habib's shoulder briefly as they walked through into the lounge.

The room was full of people. The imam was there, and Aisha's uncle Ismail and some other relations Fatimah didn't recognise. She looked over at Uncle

Ismail and couldn't stop her tears. She and Aisha had spoken about his trip to Mecca just moments before the bomb exploded. He must have cut short his pilgrimage and come back to be with the family.

Then Auntie Leila's arms were round her and they were both in tears.

'Fatimah, oh Fatimah!'

'I'm so sorry, Auntie. I'm so sorry.' It was all she could say.

Aisha's father was speaking to her. 'Thank you, Fatimah,' he said, his voice breaking with emotion. 'At least I know she was with you at the end.'

Fatimah nodded. She couldn't speak.

They stayed long enough to make sure that Aisha's family knew they would do everything they could for them, and then they left, repeating their expressions of sympathy.

'We must stand by them,' said Fatimah's father. 'We must visit them often.'

But we can't bring her back, thought Fatimah. Their lives are shattered. They will never be the same again.

'Habib has taken it badly,' said Hassan. 'He's talking of not going back to college. His dad is really worried.'

'Yes, he looks terrible,' said his mother. 'Poor boy.'

☾ ☾ ☾

The young man had been watching their house and when they left to visit Aisha's family, he crept out from where he had been hiding and made his way to the front door.

☾ ☾ ☾

They walked back to their own house in silence. Then, as they neared the front door, Hassan said, 'What's that?' He rushed forward and then stopped short. 'That's disgusting!' he shouted. 'Whoever would do a thing like that?' They stood, shocked, in the garden. Fatimah's dad put his arms around his wife and daughter as they all stared in horror.

Dog mess was smeared all over the front door.

'Quick,' he said, 'let's clear this up.'

Gingerly, he put the key in the lock and opened the door. Then he stepped back quickly.

'It's all over the hall carpet, too,' he said.

Fatimah and her mother stepped over the mess and ran into the kitchen to get a bucket of water and cleaning materials. In grim silence, they scraped and sponged and scrubbed until it was gone. But the stink lingered and there was a stain on the carpet that they couldn't get rid of, however much they rubbed at it.

Fatimah was sobbing as she worked. 'It's all my fault,' she said. 'It's because of me.'

Her mother sat back on her heels. 'Don't be ridiculous, Fatimah,' she said sharply. 'You have done nothing wrong. Dad and I are so proud of you for saving a life.'

'What else could I have done, Mum? Why are people so angry with me?'

'Because they cannot see good when it is staring them in the face.'

Fatimah said nothing more until they were alone together in the kitchen, swilling out the buckets and washing out the soiled cloths.

'Mum, there's something you should see,' she said. 'Wait there.'

Fatimah went upstairs to her room and opened a drawer. She drew out the crumpled note and took it downstairs to the kitchen, then smoothed it out and silently handed it to her mother.

Her mother read it and looked up at Fatimah, uncomprehending. 'When did this come?'

'When I came back from hospital. It was with the cards,' she said.

'But why … ? I don't understand.'

'Someone out there thinks I've been going out with a non-Muslim boy.'

'But that's not true.'

'I know it's not true, Mum, but some nutter thinks it is.'

'Have you shown this to anyone else?'

Fatimah shook her head and looked down at her feet. 'I was too ashamed,' she said.

'Let me throw it away. It's disgusting. It's worse than the mess on the door.'

Fatimah hesitated. 'Maybe we should keep it. Just in case there are more.'

'Why? What for?'

Fatimah shrugged. 'The police might want to see it.'

Her mother's shoulders drooped and she handed back the sad little piece of paper.

'Perhaps you are right. Maybe we should keep it for now, but I don't think we should show it to your father,' she said quietly.

☾ ☾ ☾

When Fatimah went to bed that night, she couldn't sleep. Whoever had smeared their door must have known that they were all out. Someone must be watching this house, she thought. Is it someone I have met? Someone who goes to the mosque? Or is it a non-Muslim, someone trying to lay the blame on our faith?

Hassan had wanted to ask his grandmother and the other neighbours if they had seen anyone, but his father had stopped him. It was too shaming, he had said. This kind of act should be ignored and treated with contempt. But it had affected them all. This was the action of a mad person. But a mad person might go on to do something worse. Where would it stop?

Fatimah lay tensed up. Her stomach was a tight ball of fear. She jumped at every noise – cars passing in the street, a motorbike backfiring, the shouts of party-goers saying goodnight.

She wondered if Steve or his family had had any threats.

Suddenly, she wanted to see him. If he was being pestered, too, then she wanted to know. Maybe they could fight it together.

The next instant, she dismissed the thought. How? How could they possibly do anything together?

☾☾☾

Steve's parents said nothing to him about the phone call. They didn't want to upset him. The police told them it had come from a local phone box and that they were studying footage from a surveillance camera in the area. But they couldn't identify anyone.

Steve was improving all the time, but he was still in

a lot of pain. Before long, the nurses had him out of bed and were teaching him to use crutches.

At first he felt as though he would never walk upright again. All the bruising had come out and, as well as his badly-broken leg, he had two black eyes, a swollen cheek and several broken ribs, but at last he managed to shuffle forward a few paces, though it was very uncomfortable and he was sweating and dizzy with the effort.

It was after one of these sessions, while he lay, exhausted, on his hospital bed, that one of the nurses came in with a note for him.

'Some more fan mail, Steve,' she said, handing it over.

Steve smiled weakly. He'd been surprised at how many people had sent him Get Well cards. He slit the envelope with his finger and pulled out a piece of paper.

The first time he read it, he didn't really take in what it meant. And then Fatimah's words came back to him: *There could be trouble for you, too, and your family.*

He smoothed it out carefully and looked at it again.

KEEP AWAY FROM THE MUSLIM GIRL
OR YOU'LL HAVE MORE BONES BROKEN

Although the room was warm and the day outside oppressive and muggy, Steve suddenly felt cold.

This is what she meant, he thought. He was furious. How dare someone write this!

Then his thoughts turned to Fatimah. Had she been getting notes like this, too?

Suddenly he really wanted to see her again. Did she want to see him, he wondered? He supposed it would be impossible for her to come and visit him, but he wished she would.

He looked at the note again. Thick black felt tip on a lined sheet of paper torn from a notepad.

'Bastards,' he muttered out loud. Then he scrunched the note up and put it in his bedside drawer. He would show it to his parents.

☾ ☾ ☾

When they arrived to visit, later that evening, Steve handed it over to them.

Ben put his hand on Steve's shoulder. 'We'll show it to the police, son,' he said grimly. Then, shifting his weight awkwardly, he continued. 'It's not true, Steve, is it? You didn't know the girl before the bombing, did you? You didn't try and chat her up?'

'Ben', said Jackie sharply. 'You know perfectly well he'd never spoken to her before that day.'

Ben made a face. 'Yeah. Well, sometimes lads don't tell their mothers everything,' he said.

'Hello,' said Steve, 'I'm here, you know. I can speak for myself.'

Jackie smiled. 'Sorry, love.'

'Don't worry, Dad,' said Steve wearily. 'I never even knew Fatimah's name before the bombing. I guess this is a threat from some nutter who thinks I might want to get to know her better.'

'And do you?' asked Jackie.

Steve frowned. She was too perceptive by half, his mum.

'Do I what?'

'Want to get to know her better?'

Ben and Jackie both watched him carefully as he tried to find the right words.

'I like her a lot, Mum, and I'll never forget what she's done for me. But I don't want to cause her any trouble.' He blushed and studied the plaster on his leg. 'Anyway, it's no good even thinking that way about Muslim girls.'

Jackie stroked the back of his hand. 'I saw her today,' she said quietly.

'What!' said Ben and Steve together.

'I went to see her and her family. You know, to say thank-you.'

'Why didn't you tell me you were going?'

asked Ben. 'You never said anything.'

'I thought it best to go on my own. I felt it would be easier.'

Ben looked hurt. 'I would have come with you.'

Jackie smiled. 'You would have found it difficult, Ben, you know you would. It was better for me to break the ice first.'

'What were they like, her family?' asked Steve.

'I didn't meet her father, but her mother and brother were there and they made me very welcome.'

'And Fatimah?'

Jackie nodded. 'Yes, she was there. She is very concerned about you. She asked me to send you her best wishes.'

Steve felt absurdly happy. Now that his mum had been to visit the family, there could perhaps be some kind of communication between them.

'They haven't had any threats or anything, have they?'

Jackie frowned. 'Well, they didn't say so – at least, not directly – but they did explain how some people in their community feel about any friendship between a Muslim girl and a non-Muslim boy, however innocent. And I told them about the phone call –' she stopped, angry with herself for mentioning it.

'What phone call?' asked Steve, frowning.

Ben interrupted. 'A crank phone call, son. We told the police and they said it happens all the time if you've had your photo in the papers.'

'Who was it on the phone? What did they say?'

Ben shrugged. 'Same sort of thing as your note: Keep away from Muslim girls.'

'It's ridiculous,' said Jackie, suddenly angry. 'We live in a free society. What harm is there in Steve going to see the family, going to thank Fatimah for saving his life?'

Steve looked at her and he knew it wasn't that simple. He was beginning to understand Fatimah's warning: Be very careful, Steve. There were people out there who didn't think like they did, people who weren't reasonable like Fatimah's family, either, people who were fanatics.

'I don't want to stir things up, Mum,' he said. 'If it's better for Fatimah and her family, then I'll keep away from them.'

'Yes. I think that's best,' said Ben quickly.

But inside, Steve was seething. Why should he give in to these threats? Perhaps if he and Fatimah stood up to them together ... let the bastards know they weren't going to be intimidated.

But what then? More violence? More vile notes? And Fatimah might be hurt.

He shifted his position on the bed and banged

his fist into his pillow.

Jackie got up and walked to the window.

'Fatimah's mother told me that the vicar from St Luke's has phoned,' she said, as she stared out of the window. 'He's been in touch with us, too.'

'Oh yeah?' said Steve, not really interested.

'You know, the papers are saying he's the reason the terrorists bombed the church – because he's been trying to set up some sort of dialogue with the local mosque.'

Steve looked up. 'What? You mean he's trying to get Muslims and Christians to do things together?'

Jackie nodded. 'The papers say he's putting himself in danger because he's working at it even harder now, since the bombing.'

She walked back across the room and took Ben's arm. 'And he's coming to visit us tomorrow evening.'

Steve grinned. 'What, the vicar? He'll have a hard job getting Dad into a church!'

'I don't think that's what he has in mind,' said Jackie.

Ben was staring at her. 'You should have asked me,' he muttered. 'You don't know where this might lead. Never mind him being in danger, what about us? It could be dangerous for us, getting involved with a bloke like that. '

His words hung in the silence, broken only by the buzzing of a sleepy fly batting against the window pane. Jackie went to the window and opened it and the fly buzzed drunkenly off to freedom.

Then she came back to Steve, kissed him on the head and picked up her bag.

'We'd better be going, love. We'll see you tomorrow.'

As soon as they left the ward, Ben exploded.

'Why? Why did you say that vicar could come?'

'Ssh,' she said. 'Because we can't bury our heads in the sand any more, that's why.' Then she changed the subject. 'And you know what to do if there are still reporters outside, don't you?'

Ben grinned suddenly, the tension broken. 'OK, OK, I know. I smile and shut up.'

'Got it in one,' said Jackie. Then, on impulse, she reached up and kissed his cheek.

'What was that for?'

'Nothing. Just felt like it.'

Ben took her hand and squeezed it. 'Love you,' he said, as they got into the lift.

'Love you too, you old dinosaur,' said Jackie, returning his squeeze.

G G G

It was Friday, and Fatimah's father and Hassan both went to noon prayers at the mosque. Hassan had no lectures in the afternoon, so he came home and for once, instead of going back to work, his father came home with him.

They arrived at the house just as Fatimah and her mother had finished their own prayers.

'Everyone at the mosque is so concerned for you, Fatimah,' said her father, 'and for Aisha's family, of course. They are all horrified at what happened.'

Not everyone, thought Fatimah, seeing again, in her mind's eye, the bold writing on the note and the dog mess smeared on the door. Some fanatic had done that. Was it the same person who had written the note? Was it a Muslim? If it was, then it was a mad extremist and someone who had probably also been at Friday prayers.

Her father was still talking. 'The imam's going to come and see us.'

'Yes, I know. You said.'

'And he wants to bring the vicar – the man at St Luke's – with him. I told him I would consider it.'

Hassan frowned and was about to say something when Fatimah's mother looked up. 'Then we should welcome them both to our home,' she said calmly, 'just as we welcomed Steve's mother.'

Fatimah's father said slowly. 'But the vicar.

The man from the church. Is this what you want? You realise what it means?'

'It means that everyone will know we approve of what he is doing – trying to build bridges,' muttered Hassan, and his mother looked at him gratefully. But he looked away, blushing. Somehow, this was too close to home. It was all very well for councillors or politicians to do this, but when there were nutters out there watching their house …

Fatimah quickly changed the subject.

'Dad,' she said. 'I really want to go back to school next week.'

Her father's expression softened and he put his arm round her shoulders. 'Do you feel ready?'

She nodded. 'I won't have my life ruined by some terrorist. I want to get back to normal.'

Her mother looked nervous. 'I don't want you walking to school on your own,' she said.

'No, ' said Fatimah, slowly. 'Perhaps Hassan …?'

'Hassan,' said their father. 'You could go to college via the school, couldn't you?'

Hassan made a face. 'Yes. I suppose so.'

Fatimah grinned. 'Just for a while, eh, Hassan? Until I feel better. And I know you'll have to get up a bit earlier.'

'OK,' he said. 'Big sacrifice, but I'll do it for you, little sister.'

So, on Monday morning, much later than usual because she had to wait for Hassan who, of course, wasn't nearly ready in time, Fatimah and Hassan started off on the familiar route.

As they turned into Aisha's road, they both fell silent.

Just as they were passing the house, the door opened and Habib came out.

'Hi,' said Hassan. 'Are you coming to college today?'

Habib nodded. 'Yeah. I'm going to give it a go.'

'Come with us, then,' said Hassan. 'I'm going to take Fatimah to school first, though.'

Habib hesitated. 'I don't think …' Then he continued. 'Sorry,' he said. 'I don't think I can face going near school. I'll catch you later.'

'Sure,' said Hassan. 'I'll see you.'

Habib turned to Fatimah. 'Thank you, Fatimah. Thank you for all you did for Aisha.'

Fatimah had felt so much stronger today, but meeting Habib's eyes for a moment, eyes so like those of his sister, she felt again all the terror she had felt on the day of the bombing. She could feel the tears coming and she turned away and looked at the ground.

'If only …' she whispered.

'Yes,' he replied. 'If only …' Then he walked away

in the opposite direction.

'Poor Habib,' she muttered.

'I don't know how to help him,' said Hassan.

'I wonder how his family will feel about the vicar coming to see us?' said Fatimah.

'What do you mean?'

'Well,' she said slowly. 'If the vicar was the reason why some madman bombed the church. How would you feel if the vicar's actions had caused my death?'

Hassan shrugged. 'But then, how does Habib feel about the bomber – the bomber who is probably a Muslim?'

Fatimah turned to face him. 'Do you believe that?'

Hassan nodded. 'I'd like to think it wasn't a Muslim, but it looks that way, from what the police are saying.'

'Oh, it's all such a muddle,' muttered Fatimah.

As they walked slowly towards the school, a germ of an idea was growing in her mind.

'Hassan,' she said, suddenly.

'Mmm.'

'I want you to come with me to the hospital. To see Steve.'

Hassan stopped abruptly. 'You're mad!'

'No. Listen to me. If you come with me, then I'm doing nothing wrong, you know that.'

'But you shouldn't, Fatimah. If you are seen ...'

'Look, Hassan. I want to be a doctor myself one day. One day I will be dealing with sick people of all races, all religions.'

'No,' said Hassan firmly. 'No, I can't allow it.'

Fatimah turned on him. 'What were you saying to Dad the other day, Hassan? You were saying it was good to talk, to discuss with your friends. To argue. To understand.'

'Yes, but ...'

'Well, don't you see? This is a chance and we should grab it. This is a chance to show that we are against violence.'

'Is that really what you want?' Hassan looked shocked, suddenly understanding what she was driving at.

Of course it is. I've never thought about it properly before now. But since the bombing ... This can't go on, Hassan. The imam and that vicar are right.'

'But have you thought what might happen if you're seen visiting Steve?'

'We've already had the dog mess, Hassan, and the note.'

'What note?'

Fatimah hesitated, then she met his eyes.

'I had a note calling me a white boy's whore,' she said, watching his face carefully. 'I told Mum but we decided not to tell you or Dad.'

Hassan clenched his fists. 'Merciful Allah.'

'So,' said Fatimah, 'it can't get much worse. Perhaps if we can help the imam and the vicar – Steve's family and our family – we can do some good.'

'You're wrong, Fatimah. It could get much worse,' said Hassan thoughtfully. 'You could get hurt. You don't understand how dangerous it could be ...'

'Oh, give me a break, Hassan. Of course I understand!'

'No. No – you can't do this!' Hassan grabbed her arm.

She shook it off. 'If you don't agree to come with me, Hassan, then I shall go on my own.'

'No! I will never allow that. Nor will Dad.'

'How will you stop me?'

'I could tell Dad.'

Fatimah faced him, her eyes furious. 'After what you said to him about being British and how good it is to talk to people of other faiths! If you go running to him to stop me trying to do exactly what you were preaching, how do you think that'll look to him? You're all talk, Hassan!'

'Yes, but it's us, our family ...'

'So you didn't really mean it? When it comes down to it, you won't stand up and be counted.'

For a long moment brother and sister looked at each other, then Hassan dropped his eyes.

'OK. I'll take you there,' he said at last. 'I suppose at least I can stop you doing anything more stupid.'

'What do you mean?'

'Nothing. Forget it. Look, we're at the school now. I'll come back and fetch you this afternoon.'

Suddenly there was a group of Fatimah's friends coming towards them, and she was swallowed up as they milled around the school gates.

Hassan stood there for a moment looking at them, then he walked slowly away.

He took a short cut through the town to get to college and, as he hurried along unfamiliar streets, he was so deep in thought that at first he didn't see the group of youths standing at a corner, nor did he realise that their shouts were directed at him.

'Terrorist!'

'Bloody Muslim!'

'Go home, Paki.'

Shocked, Hassan turned to face them. He hesitated. He could go and speak to them, reason with them – but his nerve failed. He was on his own and they looked menacing.

Then a stone hit him on the side of the face and he started to run.

CHAPTER EIGHT

Hassan was very quiet when he arrived to take Fatimah home, but she was bound up in her own thoughts, so she didn't notice his silence.

'It was good to be back,' she said at last. 'Everyone came to talk to me. All my friends – and lots of kids I'd never even met before. They were all really kind.'

'That's good,' said Hassan vaguely.

It was horrible, though, not having Aisha there,' she added quietly. 'They've … they've taken all her things away. It was as if she'd never been at school. It was as if she had never existed.' She could feel the tears coming, so she turned away and blew her nose on a tissue.

They were both quiet for a while, then Fatimah said, 'Was Habib at college?'

'I don't know. He doesn't come to many of my lectures, so I could have missed him. I hope he comes back. The longer he stays away, the harder it will be for him.'

Fatimah sighed. 'I miss Aisha every moment of the day. Imagine what it must be like for Habib and his family – for Auntie Leila.'

They were nearly home when Fatimah stopped and turned to face Hassan. 'When shall we go and see Steve?'

Hassan jerked up his head. Why on earth had he agreed to take her? In his mind's eye he saw the group of youths earlier that day giving chase as he ran away. It would be so easy to ignore the insults, keep his head down, pretend it hadn't happened, pretend that it wouldn't go on happening. Especially now, as tension was rising in the city, when everyone was suspicious. The easiest thing to do would be to keep a low profile and wait for things to calm down. He wished he'd never said all that to his father – about understanding, mutual respect, talking together. He didn't want to stand out; he wanted to merge with the crowd.

'Do you really want to go?'

'Yes, of course.'

He took a deep breath and squared his shoulders. Her words this morning had stung him. He hated being criticised, especially by a girl. OK, he wouldn't back down, but he wasn't happy.

'I'll take you there after tea,' he mumbled.

Fatimah took his arm and squeezed it gently. 'Thanks,' she said. 'You're a star.'

When they turned the corner into their street, they both looked nervously at the front door. But it was just as it always was.

Fatimah looked around her. Nothing was different. The street, the trees, the birds, the traffic. Everything was exactly as it had always been. And yet everything had changed.

Hassan put his key in the lock and pushed the door open. As they walked in, they heard the sound of voices in the lounge and they hesitated.

'Hassan, Fatimah, come in,' called their mother. 'Your father has brought the imam to see us.' Her voice sounded edgy.

As soon as they walked into the room, Fatimah realised why.

The vicar from St Luke's was there, too. He was a small, sandy-haired man with blue eyes. Beside him, the imam looked huge and swarthy, with his heavy black beard and dark eyes. Both men had just got up to leave, but the vicar came forward and Fatimah immediately sensed the strength of character in his firm handshake.

'You're a brave young woman,' he said. 'Your family must be very proud of you.'

Fatimah looked down shyly and said nothing.

He turned to her father. 'I'm sorry we can't stay longer, but we both have appointments to keep.'

As soon as they had left, Hassan said, 'What did they want?'

His father frowned. 'They have asked for our help.' He twisted his watch strap and looked at the floor.

'What kind of help?'

Fatimah's mother answered. 'Fatimah, they want you and the boy – Steve – and your families to set an example ...' Her voice faltered and she cleared her throat. 'They want to show the city that this dreadful event has brought people together, not divided them.'

Hassan thought of the group of youths pelting him with stones. He swallowed nervously.

Fatimah had gone very pale. She looked at her father. 'And what did you say, Dad?'

'I asked for time to think about it,' he said quietly. He looked from one to the other. 'It will be difficult to refuse; it is the will of the mosque committee. They have reassured me that there is no question of compromising our beliefs, but they want us to stretch out the hand of friendship.' He sighed and looked at his family, 'But if we agree, then we should all understand what this will mean.'

There was silence in the room. The clock on the

mantlepiece ticked on relentlessly.

'I don't know ...' began Hassan, breaking the silence at last.

'Isn't this what you want, son?' replied his father. 'Dialogue, understanding, mutual respect?'

'Of course,' said Hassan huskily. 'It's just ...'

'It's just that we will be doing it – our family,' said his father, 'in the full glare of publicity. Is that why you have doubts?'

Hassan didn't answer and his father continued, suddenly angry. 'So, all your fine words mean nothing when it affects you personally, Hassan. Is that it?'

Hassan looked across at Fatimah. 'No. It's just that I'm scared, Dad.'

'We are all scared, son.'

Hassan looked down at the floor. 'Some blokes threw stones at me this morning,' he muttered.

His father gripped the edge of the chair in front of him. 'Savages,' he muttered.

Fatimah interrupted. 'Then, we should try to make things better,' she said. 'We should try to help.' She looked round at her family. 'Shouldn't we?'

She watched them anxiously. One by one, they nodded unhappily, each realising what it might mean if they agreed to help. They would be off the fence and their lives would change. They would have to justify themselves, to stand up for what they had done. And there would be people who would hate them for it.

Fatimah cleared her throat. 'Hassan has agreed to take me to the hospital tonight,' she said, 'to see Steve.'

'But ...' began her father. Then he shrugged helplessly.

'If we are to help,' said Fatimah gently, 'then this is a good place to start.'

And, although she was speaking to her father, she was looking at Hassan. He held her gaze as she spoke and drew strength from its steadiness.

But their mother turned away. She couldn't bear to think of the consequences: her children's safe, ordinary, sheltered life gone for ever. Though, in reality, she knew that it had gone earlier – blown apart by the bomb.

☾ ☾ ☾

He had been well taught and the deadly package was small and unobtrusive. It would be very easy to conceal. He'd make another one for the main target – but this one had a different destination.

☾ ☾ ☾

After tea, Hassan and Fatimah set off for the hospital. Hassan had borrowed the family car and was driving carefully, his thoughts crowded. What were they getting themselves into?

They didn't speak much on the way, but when he had parked the car and they were walking towards the hospital entrance, Hassan stopped.

'Will there still be reporters?'

'Surely not,' said Fatimah. 'It's over a week since the bomb. It's old news now.'

'Not for us,' muttered Hassan grimly. Then he continued. 'What are we going to say to Steve?'

Fatimah smiled. 'Don't worry, little brother,' she said.

'Don't you "little brother" me,' he replied, but he was smiling, too.

Steve was sitting on the edge of his bed when they arrived and he looked much better.

Fatimah walked into the room first and he looked up, surprise and delight registering on his face, before he saw Hassan behind her.

'Steve, this is my brother, Hassan,' said Fatimah quickly.

'Hi. Good to meet you,' said Steve. He was furious with himself as he felt the blush rising up his neck and suffusing his cheeks.

'How are you?' said Fatimah, sitting down in the

chair by the bed. Hassan retreated towards the door and stood there awkwardly, his arms folded.

'Much better,' said Steve. 'I'm going home tomorrow.'

'Hey, that's great!'

Steve nodded. He stole a glance at Hassan and wished he'd make himself scarce. No chance of that, though, he thought. But, brother or no brother, he would speak to Fatimah – and not just about rubbish stuff.

'Fatimah,' he began, very conscious of Hassan's presence, 'has your family had a visit from that vicar?'

She nodded. 'He came with the imam this afternoon. They said they'd been to see your family, too.'

'Yeah. And you know what it's all about?'

'Yes. And Hassan and I – and our family – well, I think we're going to try and help.'

'Won't it be dangerous for you?' asked Steve. He looked across at Hassan.

Hassan cleared his throat. 'It's good you understand that,' he said quietly. 'But it will be hardest for Fatimah.'

'Hard for her to put herself in the spotlight, you mean?'

Hassan nodded. 'There'll be criticism from our community.'

'Even though the imam has asked you ...?'

'There are some people who feel that he has gone too far with this inter-faith business.'

'Hey,' interrupted Fatimah. 'Hello! I'm here too.'

'Sorry,' grinned Steve. Then he reached across for his crutches and hoisted himself off the bed and on to his feet. But he was still speaking to Hassan when he said, 'Have you had any bad stuff? Hate mail or anything?'

Fatimah looked up, startled. 'Well, yes ...' She glanced at Hassan.

Hassan gestured helplessly with his hand. 'Yes,' he said, shortly. 'Vile stuff.'

'I had a note,' said Steve, slowly. 'And there was a phone call.'

Fatimah got up from the chair and came over to Steve. 'What did the note say?' she asked, frowning. 'What was it written on?'

He looked embarrassed. 'It said to keep away from you, or else,' he muttered.

'And how did it look?' she persisted.

Steve shrugged. 'I only looked at it once, then my parents handed it over to the police. It was on lined paper, I think, torn from a notepad, and it was written in capital letters in black felt tip.'

Fatimah nodded. 'Sounds like mine,' she said.

'What did yours say?' asked Steve.

'Much the same thing,' interrupted Hassan. 'Keep away from non-Muslim boys.'

Fatimah blushed, remembering the real words: *WHITE BOY'S WHORE.*

'I've still got the note I was sent,' she said. 'I only showed it to Mum. It was filthy.'

'And we've had our front door ...' she began.

'Covered in dog shit,' finished Hassan.

'Ugh! That's revolting.'

They looked at each other.

'If we do agree to help,' said Steve, slowly, 'it's not going to stop, is it? These fanatics are going to keep on attacking us – and our families. And it'll probably get worse.'

There was an uneasy silence.

'Are you going to help?' asked Fatimah at last.

Steve looked at her steadily. 'Are you?' he asked, and dropped his eyes as he felt himself blushing again.

Hassan cleared his throat. 'Little sister, could you get me a drink of water.'

Fatimah knew that Hassan wanted her out of the way – and she knew why. But she nodded .

Hassan didn't mince his words. 'Steve,' he said quietly. 'You don't have ... have feelings for my sister, do you?'

Steve met his eyes. 'Of course I have feelings,'

he replied, enjoying the sudden flare of fury in Hassan's eyes. 'Fatimah saved my life. I owe her. For the rest of my life I shall owe her.' Then he grinned. 'But not romantic feelings, Hassan. Don't worry. I wouldn't ever go there.'

Liar! he thought to himself.

Hassan relaxed. 'Thanks for telling me that. Sorry I had to ask. It's just that...'

'I understand, mate.'

When Fatimah returned, Steve said, 'Tell me about Islam. I don't know a thing about it and if we are going to get involved in all this, maybe I should try to understand where you are coming from. And then I could try and explain to my dad,' he said, making a face as he thought of Ben's likely reaction.

So Hassan and Fatimah started to explain all that Islam meant to them and to their family. Frowning, Steve concentrated carefully, sometimes questioning, but mostly just listening.

'Yeah. I see there's a lot of good in it,' he said at last, biting his lip and choosing his words carefully, 'but some of the rules and laws – they go back so far! The world's a different place now.'

'If the laws are good, why should they change?' asked Hassan, quoting exactly his father's views when he'd questioned him.

'But surely, don't some of them need to adjust?'

said Steve. He knew he was treading on sensitive ground and he didn't want to blow it.

He's picking up on all the points I've raised with Dad, thought Hassan. And I'm putting forward all Dad's arguments!

He turned the conversation round.

'What about you, Steve?' he said. 'What is your faith?'

Steve looked uncomfortable. 'I don't come from a religious family,' he mumbled. 'So I've never had any faith.'

'What – nothing? Don't you believe in anything?' said Fatimah. She thought back to the visit from Steve's mum. She seemed such a nice, caring person. Fatimah was surprised that she had no faith.

Steve tugged at his ear. No one had ever asked him this before.

He frowned. 'Well, yes. Sure. I believe... I believe in being loyal to my mates, I suppose... and honest ... and kind... and all that sort of stuff...' He trailed off.

Fatimah smiled. 'I can't imagine not having my faith,' she said simply.

Steve was silent for a while, then he said, 'but Fatimah, don't you... don't you sort of resent the fact that men are so much more important in your faith?'

Fatimah snorted. 'You don't believe that, do you? Sure, men have their role, but so do women.

And being a Muslim girl isn't going to stop my education or my career.'

'But ... but as a girl you seem to have no freedom.'

Hassan clenched his fists angrily, but Fatimah looked across at him and frowned.

'I think I am really free, Steve. I know exactly what the rules are and that is very liberating. Most of the non-Muslim girls at school, they don't know where to stop. They don't have boundaries. And it doesn't make them happy. They're just confused.'

Hassan looked away. He admired her unwavering devotion to Islam but, not for the first time, he had to push down his doubts. He wasn't so sure of anything any more.

Steve was more puzzled than ever. None of the girls he knew would tolerate living under the rules which Fatimah seemed so easy with. But one thing was for sure. It was a part of her and it made her the person she was – the person he felt close to and wanted to know better.

C C C

That night, as Fatimah was going to bed, she took out the crumpled note from her chest of drawers, where she had hidden it. She carried it over to her desk and gingerly smoothed it out. Then she held it up to the lamp. Perhaps, like Steve, she should hand it over to the police.

But she didn't want her father to know, and she hated the thought of the police seeing what had been written about her.

If it was from the same notepad as Steve's note, then surely, if there were any clues about who had sent it, they'd get it from his note. They didn't need hers as well.

She stared at it long and hard, less frightened by it now, less disgusted. It was as if, by sharing the experience with Steve, the note's vicious words were put into perspective.

She was about to put it away again when she turned it over. She frowned. Then she felt the paper with the tips of her fingers. There was a slight indentation. She sat back and thought: Was something written on the notepad before this message? Was something written on the page on top of my note and then torn off?

She laid the note face down and felt the raised letters again. They must have been written in pencil or biro and the writer must have been pressing hard. She rummaged in her desk drawer until she found a thick pencil. Very carefully, she drew the pencil back and forth over the raised bits and then peered again.

Yes! There was something there, but whatever

it was looked back to front. She walked over to the mirror on the wall and held the paper up to it. It was too dark to make out, so she dragged the lamp from her desk over to the mirror. Her heart beat a little faster. They were numbers! Numbers and a rough drawing of some sort.

Painstakingly, she drew exactly what she saw in the mirror on to a fresh sheet of paper.

She stared at the numbers and the drawing for ages, but nothing made any sense to her. She'd show it to Hassan tomorrow, see if it meant anything to him. If it did, then perhaps …

She sighed, rubbed her sore eyes and headed for bed. She looked at her clock. One o'clock in the morning!

She dropped the paper back into her chest of drawers and, as she did, she saw the scarf lying there, the scarf she had bought for Aisha, for Eid. She took it out gently and held it against her cheek. She prayed for Aisha every day. Her lovely friend. Aisha's loss was an ache which would never go away. She turned off the lights and padded over to the window, still clutching the scarf. She needed some air.

But as she opened the window, she stiffened.

It was only the faintest noise, but it wasn't the hum of traffic or the sound of a breeze in the garden shrubs. She listened, every sense alert. There was something. Someone was there. Someone was in their front garden!

Fatimah stood rigid by the open window. Could she be seen? She didn't think so. It was a cloudy night and there was no moon. The only light came from the street lamp on the pavement. Her heart was beating fast and the palms of her hands felt sweaty. She kept absolutely still as she stared into the garden, her eyes slowly adjusting to the darkness.

Nothing. No sound at all. Not even a leaf stirring. But still she didn't move. Then, gradually, as her eyes adjusted to the dark, she spotted a figure walking slowly down the street, slinking along beside the fences and walls and hedges that edged the front gardens of the houses. At first, all she could make out was the dark, shadowy movement, and then the shadows firmed up into a figure. A completely silent figure, edging forward, slowly and carefully.

She knew, instinctively, that the person was going to stop at their gate. She started to shiver, but she stayed where she was, watching from the crack between the closed curtains of her bedroom window.

Even from a distance, she could see that the person was dressed in dark clothes and had a backpack. And she was sure, now, that it was a man. She watched as he glanced up and down the street. Then, seeing no one about, he opened the gate and crept up the path towards their front door, shrugging his backpack off as he went.

I must tell Dad! thought Fatimah. But just as she was about to run and wake her parents, another figure emerged from the bushes.

She stared, horrified.

The second person crept up behind the first and grabbed the backpack. The first man swung round, fists raised. But then he recognised the second man and there was a whispered conversation.

Fatimah waited no longer. She turned and ran but, as she did so, she tripped on the rug and cried out as she tried to save herself from falling. She scrambled to her feet and quickly went back to the window again. The two men were running away down the street as silently as they had come.

Shaking with fear, Fatimah ran into her parents' room.

Her mother was awake at once, holding her, stroking her hair, comforting her. As soon as they'd heard what had happened, her father rang the police and they came round at once. All the movement in the house had woken Hassan, too, and he came stomping down the stairs into the kitchen, rubbing his eyes and asking what all the fuss was about.

But Fatimah could tell the police very little, and after asking a lot of questions and taking a lot of notes, they went away, promising to have the house guarded and saying that a team would be back to search the garden in daylight.

Fatimah's father had protested. 'We don't want attention focused on our home, on our family,' he said. But the police had been firm. 'This is a security matter, sir. I'm afraid you have no choice.'

Huddled together in the hall, the family saw the police out.

'Perhaps I should have said nothing,' muttered Fatimah.

'Don't be stupid, Fatimah,' said Hassan. 'Those nutters were probably trying to kill us.'

Their mother's eyes widened. 'Surely not!'

Hassan shrugged. 'Who knows what was in that backpack. It could have been anything.'

It could have been a bomb, thought Fatimah.

There was little point in going back to bed; no one felt like sleeping.

So, for once, they said the first prayers of the day together at sunrise, and even Hassan was quiet as his father prayed to Allah for peace to be restored to their family and their city.

Later, as Fatimah was getting ready for school, she glanced out of her window again. It was a perfect, still, early summer's day. Heavy-eyed with lack of sleep, she stared into the garden and, in her mind's eye, saw again those two figures running away down the street.

She frowned. I'm missing something here, she thought. There's a connection I'm not making.

She went to her desk and drew out the tracing she had made from the lined notepad.

But, however much she stared at them, the numbers and the drawing still made no sense to her, so she sighed and put the paper back.

☾ ☾ ☾

They were running along the road in the dark – two figures in dark clothes.

'Why did you do that? Why did you stop me?'

'You know why. He said not to draw attention to ourselves. We wait for the big one.'

CHAPTER NINE

Steve, too, was staring out of the window at the cloudless sky. He was dressed and ready to go home. He couldn't wait to get out of hospital.

At last Ben came to fetch him.

'Isn't Mum coming?'

Ben shook his head. 'She sends her love, but there's this big meeting at work she really needs to be at.' He paused. 'We've both taken a lot of time off work ... we can't ...'

He didn't finish the sentence and Steve saw the strain in his face.

'Yeah, sure. I understand.'

Ben plonked a large plastic bag on the bed.

'You won't believe the security checks downstairs,' he said. 'They took everything out of this bag.'

'What's in it?'

'Presents for the nurses,' said Ben. 'Chocolates and things. And,' he said, drawing something out with a flourish, 'I got you this!'

He thrust a mobile phone towards Steve. Steve adjusted his crutches and took it.

'Hey, Dad! This is a really good one. The latest.' He grinned. 'Bet you didn't choose this yourself!'

'I did. The young lad in the shop was a real help, though.'

'Thanks. That's brilliant!'

They said goodbye to all the nurses and handed out the presents, then made their way down to the entrance.

When they reached the reception desk, Ben left Steve on his own while he went to fetch the car.

Steve's SIM card had been saved from the bombing. He put it into his new phone and spent the next few minutes getting the phone up and running. Then he rummaged in his bag and found the scrap of paper where Hassan had written his number. He added this to the address list.

Then, on impulse, he punched the call button. He was quite relieved when the voice mail kicked in. He wanted to leave the ball in Hassan's court.

'Hi, Hassan. It's Steve here. Just to say I've got a new mobile now. Give me a call sometime.'

He hesitated. 'I'd like to meet up ... OK. Bye for now.'

Ben was soon back. Steve shuffled through the

automatic doors and out into the sunshine. For a moment he stood still, blinking in the strong light and filling his lungs with fresh air.

Ben was beside him and Steve turned to smile at him, relieved to be out of hospital, relieved to be going home, relieved to be alive.

Then the moment was shattered by the flash of a camera. A reporter had emerged from nowhere.

'Pleased to be going home, Steve?' he asked. 'What do you feel about the people who did this to you? Are you going to see that lovely Muslim girl again?'

The questions kept coming, one after the other.

How the hell did they know I was coming out of hospital today? thought Steve.

Ben took his arm protectively. 'Don't say a thing,' he hissed urgently into his ear. But Steve hesitated. What would she want me to do? he thought. What would she want me to say?'

Then he turned to the reporter and looked him in the eyes.

'Yeah,' he said slowly. 'I'm really glad to be going home.'

'And what about the bomber?' persisted the reporter.

Steve could feel his father's fingers digging into his arm. He thought quickly. He mustn't say anything stupid.

'I wish I could understand what would make someone do something like that,' he said.

There were more flashes, more questions, but Ben was hurrying him away. In a moment, he had opened the back door of the car and was manhandling Steve, helping him to lie across the back seat with his leg stretched out and his crutches on the floor.

But just before the door shut, another question floated through the air at them.

'What about the girl?'

Steve kept his eyes on the floor of the car and his mouth shut. Then Ben started the engine and they were on their way home.

Even the short car journey exhausted Steve. Although his ribs were mending and his bruising had subsided, every application of the brakes, every turn, any stopping and starting, jolted his body with waves of pain. When at last they reached home, he felt faint and sore. Ben helped him out of the car and into the house.

They had made up a bed downstairs for him so he didn't have to go up and down the stairs on his crutches. Later, Jackie came in from work and after they'd had tea, Steve went thankfully to bed. He fell asleep almost immediately, despite the discomfort from his leg and ribs. It was really good to be at home, away from the constant clatter of ward life and the relentless routine of nurses' checks and doctors' rounds. His parents crept round him and let him sleep, then they, too, headed for bed.

It was very early in the morning when Steve woke. For a moment he didn't know where he was, then his brain adjusted and he knew, and relaxed.

He lay still for a while, trying to ignore the stiffness and pain that had come over him during the night. Then, reluctantly, he heaved himself up, shuffled to the edge of the bed and reached for the glass of water and painkillers which were beside the bed.

'Damn,' he muttered, as he knocked the glass flying. 'Clumsy idiot.' Sighing, he stretched out for his crutches. Nothing for it, he would have to get more water or he wouldn't be able to swallow the pills.

It took him a long time to get upright. The bed at home was much lower than the hospital bed, but at last he was on his feet. He didn't bother to switch on the light. He didn't want to disturb his parents; if they knew he was up, Jackie would be down in an instant, fussing over him and he didn't want that.

Slowly, bit by bit, he made his way across the lounge and into the kitchen. He filled his glass and swallowed the pills. Then he filled the glass again and started to make his way back to bed, trying to shuffle on one crutch and balance the water in his free hand. It was hard work and he spilt a lot of water along the way; he had to go through the front hall to get back to the lounge and, for a moment, he stood in the kitchen doorway to catch his breath and balance the water more securely.

As he stood there, his leg throbbing with pain, summoning up the energy to hop his way back to bed, he heard a movement outside the front door.

At first he thought he had imagined it. He frowned and kept absolutely still.

No. He hadn't imagined it. There it was again. Someone was there. He stared at the front door, his heart thumping, waiting for another sound, another movement. Then slowly the letterbox was pushed open and something fell inside on to the hall mat. It was a package – and it was alight!

Steve had no time to think. Swinging forward on his crutch, he tossed the glass of water over the burning mass on the doormat. Then he switched on the light and headed into the kitchen again, snatched the nearest container – a jug – and, with trembling hands, filled it with water, shouting all the time for his parents.

The glass of water had little effect. The fire was still burning. He flung the jug of water at it, which quenched it for a moment, then it flared up again.

The noise had woken Ben and Jackie and he heard movement from upstairs.

'Dad!' he yelled, 'Quick, get the fire extinguisher!'

Ben snatched the extinguisher from the wall as he came down. He didn't pause, but aimed the jet at the burning heap. Again and again it flared up but then, at last, the fire died.

Jackie was standing at the bottom of the stairs, her hands covering her mouth. She looked from Ben to Steve.

'Oh my God,' she whispered.

Ben put down the extinguisher. Steve moved forward to look at the smouldering heap.

'Don't go near it!' said Ben harshly. 'Leave it alone.'

Then he went to the phone in the hall and dialled the police.

They hardly spoke as they sat, huddled together, in the lounge.

The police came quickly. They took statements, made reassuring noises and told them that Fatimah's home had been targeted, too. They promised to put a guard on the house.

'Oh no, surely that's not necessary, is it?' said Jackie.

Ben squeezed her hand. 'Better that, than have the family attacked, love.'

'But they can't guard us for ever. What then?' Jackie's voice was shrill with fright and fatigue.

No one answered.

Steve looked at her and Fatimah's words kept going round and round in his head: *Be careful. Be very careful.*

He'd never felt like this before, never known what it was to be hated. Until now he'd been anonymous, just another teenager living in an ordinary house in a big city, hanging out with friends, doing all the things teenagers do. Now someone hated him. Someone was watching him.

It was a horrible feeling. As he lay on his bed, trying to catch an hour's sleep as dawn rose over the city, he started at every sound, however small. Time crawled by, and at last his parents came down and started their morning routine. Jackie looked shattered. Steve heard them whispering together in the kitchen.

'I feel bad about leaving him on his own, but I can't take more time off work.'

'Don't be daft. There's a police guard here now. It's quite safe.'

Steve heaved himself up to a sitting position. 'I can hear you!' he shouted through to the kitchen.

Jackie came in and Steve gave her a weak smile.

'I'll be fine, Mum, don't worry.'

They fussed over him at breakfast and made him promise not to leave the house.

It's like being in prison, he thought.

He was relieved when they'd both gone to work. He watched them from the window. On the way out, they stopped to talk to the policeman at the gate.

How long will this go on? he thought. They can't protect us for ever. And what then? Will we always have to live with this fear hanging over us? Fear of an unknown, faceless enemy?

He read for a while. He should be revising. There had been talk of him postponing his exams for a year, but he couldn't stand the thought of two more years at school so he was going to take them, bad leg or no bad leg.

But he couldn't concentrate on his books. He kept seeing Fatimah's face. He wanted to see her so much. It was a worse ache than the pain in his leg.

He took his mobile from his pocket. Hassan hadn't got back to him yet and he didn't want to push it. Then, as he was holding the mobile, it rang. He pressed the key and slammed it against his ear.

'Hi, Hassan. How are you doing?'

There was a pause and Steve held his breath. Hassan couldn't invade his thoughts, could he? He didn't realise how much Steve cared for Fatimah, did he?

To break the silence, Steve said. 'Someone tried to set fire to our house last night.'

It was a bit over-dramatic, but it certainly got Hassan's attention.

'What?'

'Yeah,' said Steve. 'Lucky I was awake, otherwise it could have done real damage.' And he explained what had happened.

'That's terrible,' said Hassan. Then he added, 'We had people in the garden last night but Fatimah saw them and they ran away.'

'Things can't go on like this,' said Steve quietly.

'No.' There was another pause, then Hassan said, 'Look, the imam and that vicar man, they want to get together with all of us now. With everyone in both our families.'

Steve's heart leapt. A chance to see Fatimah again! He tried to keep his voice level. 'Yeah? Well, what do you think?'

Hassan hesitated. 'It might make things worse,' he said slowly.

'How?'

'I don't know. Say they want us to go public, to say something to the papers or the television. Tell the media that we are working together or something. Give the idea that young Muslims and non-Muslims have lots in common. It could mean more bad stuff from people who want to keep us apart.'

'But we've always known that,' said Steve. Oh please don't back out now, Hassan, he thought, seeing his chance of meeting Fatimah slipping away. He closed his eyes and tried to think clearly, before he replied.

'Hassan, if we see them, we don't have to agree to anything. We can always refuse to say anything in public.' He paused. 'It depends what they want us to do, doesn't it?'

'Yeah. Well, the mosque committee and the imam are in favour, so I expect they'll persuade my dad to say yes,' said Hassan. Then he continued, 'Can you ask your parents about it, Steve? Ask them if they'll meet up with my family and the imam and the vicar all together?'

'Sure,' said Steve. 'I can get hold of them at work.'

Steve rang off. He felt absurdly happy. He must persuade his parents that it was a good thing to go along with this. To meet up, at least. He couldn't wait to see Fatimah again!

When Steve rang and told them, Jackie said yes at once, but Ben was non-committal and said he wanted to talk about it when he got home.

Steve mooched about the house, occasionally staring out at the policeman. At one point, to break the monotony, he opened the window and asked him if he wanted a drink. It took Steve ages to make a mug of tea and even longer to limp, on one crutch, down the garden path and deliver it. But he felt incredibly pleased with himself afterwards, even though it had cost him an enormous effort and he was panting and sweating when he got back inside the house.

Time passed agonisingly slowly. Steve tried texting some of his friends, but they were all at school with their mobiles switched off. He dozed in front of the television but switched it off when, yet again, the news featured the police search for the bomber.

At least they haven't mentioned the attacks on our homes, he thought. At least that's been kept out of the news.

At last, he heard the key in the door and Ben was home, followed about half an hour later by Jackie. Steve tried not to confront them straight away about the proposed meeting. He waited until they had finished tea and then brought up the subject.

'I don't think we should get too involved,' said Ben. 'We don't know where all this is going.'

'So you just want to bury your head in the sand,' snapped Jackie. 'Pretend there isn't a problem and ignore it, when you're in a position to help.'

Ben sighed. 'I just don't think it will solve anything,' he said, rubbing his forehead.

'Couldn't we find out what they want from us,

at least?' said Steve. 'They may not want us to do anything.'

'Why are you so keen to do this?' asked Ben, looking straight at Steve.

Steve felt the familiar blush colouring his cheeks. He hoped his dad couldn't read his thoughts.

He spoke slowly. 'I would have died if Fatimah hadn't helped me,' he said. 'I think we should at least meet with her family and the imam and the vicar and hear what they have to say. If her family are up for it, then I think we should be, too.'

Ben glanced at Jackie.

'I agree with Steve,' she said. 'I think it's cowardly not to meet up with them all.'

Inside, Steve was shouting with triumph, but he kept his voice very calm. 'We don't have to agree to anything they suggest, Dad.'

Ben heaved himself out of his chair, walked over to the telly and turned it on. He didn't answer.

☾ ☾ ☾

'Not long now,' said the older man. 'You know what to do?'

The younger man nodded. 'Yes.'

'Then tell me again. Step by step. Minute by minute. We don't want any mistakes.'

CHAPTER TEN

The meeting between the families, the imam and the vicar was set up for the following evening. They decided to meet at Steve's home so that he wouldn't have to travel.

All day, Steve was nervous. Nervous of what Fatimah would think of his home, nervous of meeting her mother and father, and specially nervous of what Ben would say or do and how Fatimah would react to him.

He practised walking up and down the garden on his crutches, eyeing the policeman at the gate, irritated by his presence, but reassured, too. He tried to revise, he listened to music, watched the telly, played a few computer games. But all the time he was thinking about the evening to come.

If they all agreed to get involved with whatever it was that these two men were planning, what would it mean?

By the time Jackie came back from work, Steve was in a state.

'Calm down, for goodness sake,' she said, as she plonked some shopping on the kitchen table and started to put it away.

Steve picked up a packet of pasta from the table and started to fiddle with it.

'What if Dad says something awful?' he said suddenly. 'I know he wouldn't mean to, but it might come out all wrong.'

Jackie frowned. 'Give him some credit, Steve. He knows how important this is. He's not going to muck it up.'

'But what if …'

'We won't get anywhere if we all pussyfoot around. Everyone needs to air their views.' She paused. 'Dad's views are as valid as anyone else's. And they're probably the views of a lot of other people in this country.'

Steve was shocked. 'I thought you disagreed with him.'

'I understand where he's coming from, love. And I'm sure that Fatimah and her family and their friends would, too, if they put themselves in our place.'

She took the pasta from him and put it on the shelf over the cooker.

'Dad's not a bigot, Steve. It's just that he's not come across many Muslims. He's scared of what he doesn't understand. And I think it's great that he's prepared to do this – to meet up and talk.'

Steve didn't answer. He shifted in his chair.

She went on. 'It's not about us, love. It's much bigger than that.'

Jackie pulled up a chair and sat down beside him. Steve saw that her lip was trembling. She put her hands up to her face.

'Mum,' he said, putting his hand on her arm. 'Mum, don't cry.'

She took her hands away from her face and sniffed. Then she looked him full in the face.

'You nearly died, Steve. And it could happen again – to anyone. We're dealing with fanatics here.'

They were both quiet for a bit, then Steve said, 'What do you think they'll ask us to do?'

Jackie shrugged. 'I expect they have a plan. Anyway, don't let's talk about it any more. Let's just wait and see. And, meanwhile, what shall I give them to drink? Fatimah's family won't drink alcohol, will they?'

Steve shook his head. 'No, just soft drinks, I guess.' He paused. 'Perhaps you and Dad could have soft drinks, too.'

Jackie rounded on him. 'No, Steve. I'll have a glass

of wine and Dad will have a beer. As usual. We want them to see us as we are, not pretending to be what we're not.'

Steve watched her put the rest of the food away and their talk drifted to other topics, both consciously avoiding what was really on their minds.

When Ben came in they had tea, then they waited for Fatimah's family, the imam and the vicar to arrive.

'I hope that vicar won't try to get me into church,' muttered Ben.

'Oh, for heaven's sake, Ben. He's got more important things on his mind!'

At last there was a ring on the doorbell. Steve tensed up and reached for his crutches to stand up. Ben jumped up nervously and stood uncertainly in the middle of the lounge.

And Jackie smoothed back her hair and walked calmly to the front door.

When everyone was inside, the room seemed very full. For a while, they made small-talk about school and college, about jobs and houses, and Jackie and Ben served out drinks and bits and pieces to nibble. Jackie was relieved when the vicar accepted a glass of beer.

Steve had put himself next to Hassan on the sofa, and he looked across at Fatimah sitting on a chair between her parents. She smiled at him and their eyes met briefly before she looked down at her hands in her lap. Steve knew he had a dopey smile on his face, but he couldn't help it. Couldn't wipe it off.

Although Fatimah was wearing her hijab, some of her glossy black hair had escaped and to Steve she looked more gorgeous than ever. He tore his eyes away and tried to concentrate on what the others were saying.

The vicar explained how he and the imam had been working together for some time, trying to get people of different faiths – different backgrounds – to talk to each other, to meet and do things together so that there could be more mutual understanding.

Steve's parents were listening carefully and so were Fatimah's.

Then the imam spoke, backing up all the vicar had said. When the imam had finished, Ben cleared his throat. Steve clenched his fists, willing him not to say anything stupid.

'Can you explain to us,' began Ben, slowly, 'why it is that some fanatics do these terrible things? What are they trying to prove?'

'First of all,' said the imam, 'let me say that most Muslims living in this country are totally, totally against violence. But there are some young men who are influenced by the teachings of radical clerics, both in this country and abroad.'

'So, what are these teachings?' asked Ben.

And suddenly, Steve's heart went out to his father. He could see how hard he was trying to understand something completely outside his own experience, utterly alien to his own nature.

The vicar spoke up. 'Correct me if I'm wrong,' he said, turning to the imam, 'but I think there are some passages in the Koran which can be interpreted to mean that any non-believer should be killed – and some fanatics justify their actions by quoting these.'

The imam nodded. 'You must understand that nothing has been changed in the Koran and that it was written down hundreds and hundreds of years ago. We believe it is the word of God, dictated to the prophet Mohammed, and taken by Muslims to be the final word.'

'So, some of these passages ...' began Jackie.

'Some of these passages refer to a very different age,' said the imam, nodding. 'And some radical Muslims believe that the lifestyle led in this country and in others is decadent and that people who live these lifestyles should be enlightened. They believe – quite wrongly in my view – that people can be frightened into changing their way of life.'

'Of course they can't,' blurted out Ben. 'Violence just makes things worse.'

Fatimah's father was nodding. 'I absolutely agree,'

he said quietly. 'We have a well-ordered faith and we believe that it is the right way to live. But we want to live peacefully with our neighbours and we want to respect them. Though sometimes,' he added quietly, 'it is difficult to do this.'

'And we want to understand them,' said Hassan, quickly. He turned to Ben. 'It's easier for me, because I'm at college with lots of non-Muslims and I discuss things with them. We may think differently, but we can still be friends.'

Gradually, the two clerics, Steve's parents and Fatimah's parents started to relax and the conversation flowed naturally.

For a while Steve, Hassan and Fatimah listened politely and even contributed every now and again. But Steve was desperate to speak to Fatimah. He knew he couldn't see her on her own, but if it had to be with Hassan present, then that would have to do.

He turned to Hassan. 'Let's go outside,' he said. 'I've been in the house all day.'

Hassan nodded. 'You coming, Fatimah?' he said.

Fatimah hesitated. She glanced at her father, who was engrossed in conversation. 'Yes, sure,' she replied, getting up and following the boys out into the garden.

That was easy, thought Steve, as he swung towards the door on his crutches. He hadn't thought he'd be able to get her away from her parents. Once in the garden, it was obvious that Hassan and Fatimah were anxious to speak to him, too. Steve sat on the bench at the end of the back garden and the others sat on the ground in front of him.

'We've got something to show you,' said Hassan, without preamble.

Fatimah took a piece of paper from the pocket of her trousers. She unfolded it and gave it to Steve. Steve stared at it, uncomprehending.

'Does it mean anything to you?' she asked.

He shook his head. 'It's just a doodle,' he said. 'A sort of shield thing and then a whole lot of numbers.'

Hassan looked disappointed. 'It doesn't mean anything to us, either,' he said.

Steve frowned. 'What is it? Where did it come from?'

Fatimah looked away from him. 'I traced it off the back of that note I was sent,' she said.

'The note like the one I had?'

She nodded. 'Someone must have written something on the sheet above it and pressed hard enough for it to come through.'

Steve looked again, from every angle, willing the scribbles to mean something. 'No, sorry,' he said at last. 'It doesn't mean a thing to me.' He shifted his weight on the seat and went on. 'Did you hand your note over to the police?'

'No,' said Fatimah. 'I didn't want my father to see it. And if I'd given it to the police, he would have had to know about it. Do you think I should have given it to them?'

Steve shrugged. 'I dunno. The police haven't got anywhere with my note. It came from a standard notepad and the felt tip could have come from anywhere. And it was posted locally. But that's all they can find out about it.'

They sat there in the garden chatting for some time, until Fatimah's parents and Steve's mum and dad came out to join them.

'The others have just gone,' said Jackie.

'Did you decide anything?' asked Steve, looking up at her.

Fatimah's father spoke. 'We said that we would all help – if we can,' he said slowly.

'So, what does that mean?' asked Hassan. 'What will we be expected to do?'

'They want to set up some sort of working party, I think, made up of families from all sorts of backgrounds who are against violence,' said Ben.

'Sounds a bit vague,' said Steve, frowning.

'Yes, well, it is. It's going to build on what they've got already with the inter-faith thing,' said Ben.

'But you don't have any faith,' Steve blurted out.

Jackie interrupted. 'That's not really the point,' she said. 'They want to get lots of families together, from whatever background. Not just those who are committed Christians or Muslims.'

'So, who's going to join, then, apart from us?' asked Hassan.

'They will make some sort of announcement about it when they are ready,' said his mother. She hesitated. 'And they want Aisha's family to be involved, too, right at the beginning.'

Fatimah looked down at the ground. Any mention of Aisha made her miserable. I owe it to her, she thought. I owe it to Aisha to do this.

They all talked for a little longer, then everyone drifted into the house. Steve was bringing up the rear, awkward on his crutches, and Fatimah waited for him.

It's now or never, he thought. And, as they were going through the door together, into the house, Steve reached for Fatimah's hand and squeezed it.

She didn't pull it away, but squeezed his hand gently in return.

Joy exploded through Steve and a huge grin lit up his face. Fatimah smiled at him.

She squeezed my hand and she's smiling at me! he thought. How little that was, and yet how much.

Any of his friends would think he was daft, getting so excited about such a tiny demonstration of affection.

But it meant everything to him.

C C C

In bed that night, Fatimah tossed and turned. She knew there was a watch on their house and that no one could harm the family, but she was still scared.

She kept thinking about Steve. She couldn't deny it any longer. She fancied him. She had never even thought of a non-Muslim boy this way before and she knew it could only lead to trouble, but it was a fact. He was funny and he wasn't small-minded, either. He really wanted to know about her way of life and to understand her and her family.

She liked him. She liked him a lot.

She looked at her hand and remembered the feeling when he had held it – only for a moment, but she knew then that he felt the same way about her.

She sighed. Life had been so simple until that horrible bomb went off.

C C C

Steve couldn't sleep either, so he gave up trying. He took the piece of paper that Fatimah had given him and looked at it again:

The outline of a crudely drawn shield with some numbers in it: 1 8 8 5. And then, below that, some other numbers jotted down, followed by an exclamation mark.

He frowned and stared, uncomprehending. Then he tossed the paper away angrily.

There was a heap of books on his desk. The exams started in two weeks and he knew he should be revising, but his mind hadn't taken anything in these few last days. He picked up one of his exercise books and stared at the cover. He was far too tired to study, anyway. Perhaps tomorrow he would feel better.

He was just putting the book down when he noticed something. The book had the crest of the school on the front – a shield with the school motto inside it and a date – the date the school was built. Every one of their exercise books was the same.

His head jerked up. Suddenly he was fully awake.

A shield – with numbers inside! There was a shield on Fatimah's note, too. A shield with numbers inside. Could they be a date? A date when something was built?

1 8 8 5. Could that be the year 1885?

1885 was a date in Victorian times, when a lot of the important buildings in the city had been built.

But why would anyone draw the shield with the date in it? What could it mean? Steve chewed his nails and stared, unseeing, at the floor, his brain working overtime.

Unless ... unless one of those important buildings was going to be a target. A target for the people who had left the bomb in the church. Another target for the terrorists.

His heart started to beat faster as he picked up the paper again.

The numbers below the shield swam before his eyes, but an idea was forming in his mind. Could these numbers, too, refer to a date?

He could easily be wrong. It was probably nothing. But if he was right ...

He took some deep breaths and then looked again at the numbers below the shield.

103035

If that meant what he thought it meant, then time was running out.

Steve picked up his mobile and started to dial the special number they had for the police. Then he stopped. Fatimah didn't want her father to see that note. If Steve involved the police, they would want to know where he'd got the numbers from and he'd have to tell them about it. But surely this was more important than keeping the note from Fatimah's father? Wasn't it?

He frowned and stared at the mobile in his hand. This was dynamite! He hesitated. He would have to be very careful what he said over the phone. If the terrorists knew where he lived, they might be able to intercept phone calls and they'd know he'd discovered something. He couldn't risk it. If they got any inkling that he knew their next target, then there would be no chance of finding out who they were.

Fatimah's words came back to him again: *Be very careful, Steve.*

He switched the phone off and put it down on his desk. Then he logged on to the internet.

He typed in the name of his town and the word 'architecture'.

CHAPTER ELEVEN

It was very late indeed by the time Steve had finished. He had printed out several sheets of paper, and in places the writing on them was circled or there were notes in the margin. He crawled into bed and slept fitfully, but he was awake soon after dawn and struggled into his clothes and limped into the kitchen before his parents were up.

As he reached into the fridge for some juice, he glanced at the clock. How soon could he phone Hassan?

He ached all over from lack of sleep, from being hunched over the computer with his bad leg stretched out at an awkward angle. And his stomach was knotted with tension.

Jackie came down first. She saw his drawn face.

'Bad night?' she asked.

Steve nodded. He felt that he might betray himself if he said anything to her. He longed to confide in her, to tell her what he thought he'd discovered. But if he did that – if he told his parents – they would be sure to get the police involved right away, and he wanted Fatimah to know first. She'd trusted him enough to tell him about the note. She'd have to agree to show it to the police.

He must speak to Hassan.

He refused breakfast and went back into the lounge. He phoned Hassan's mobile.

Please answer, he thought, as the ringing tone went on.

Then, at last, a breathless voice on the other end.

Steve came straight to the point.

'Hassan, can you come over?'

'Well, yeah, I suppose so. When? After college?'

'No. Now.' Steve kept his voice low.

'No, I can't, mate. I've got lectures …'

'It's really important,' said Steve, his voice almost a whisper.

'What's it about?'

'I can't say. Just come, please. Right away.'

And, before Hassan could answer, Steve hung up.

Please God, let him come, he thought.

His mobile rang and he saw that it was Hassan's number on the screen. Steve didn't answer and let the voicemail kick in.

Hassan and Fatimah were walking to school when Steve rang.

When she heard it was Steve, Fatimah stopped walking for a moment, then fell into step beside Hassan.

After the phone went dead, Hassan tried calling back.

'What's the matter? What's he ringing you for?' asked Fatimah.

Hassan frowned. 'I don't know. He sounded really stressed. He wants me to go over there, now.'

'Now?'

Hassan shrugged. 'I can't go. I've got to see you to school and I've got a lecture this morning.'

Fatimah tugged at his sleeve. 'Stop, Hassan! I think we should go. Maybe ... maybe he's got something to tell us.'

'Surely it can wait, can't it?'

Fatimah took his hand. 'Look, he wouldn't have rung if he didn't need to see us.'

'Us?'

Fatimah nodded. 'I'm coming too.'

'Don't be stupid, Fatimah. You've got school – and exams next week. You can't take time off now!'

Fatimah stamped her foot in exasperation. 'If it's that important, I want to be there. I want to know what it's all about. And in any case, I've done all the revising I can. Any more, and I'll explode.'

Hassan looked at her and raised an eyebrow.

She smiled. 'Er … sorry. Bad choice of words!'

'What would Dad say?' he said at last.

'He doesn't need to know.' She took her mobile from her schoolbag and made a call.

'There,' she said. 'I've told them I'll be in later. Let's go.'

'No!'

But Fatimah had already turned round and was walking quickly in the opposite direction. Hassan ran to catch up with her. He took her arm but she shook him off and wheeled round to face him. Her expression was set and determined and Hassan bit back the remark he was going to make, shrugged, and fell into step beside her.

They didn't speak much as they made their way to Steve's house, but when they got there and saw the policeman at the gate, they hesitated.

'What shall we say?' said Fatimah.

'The truth, I guess. Just say we've come to see how Steve is.'

The policeman looked at them, suspicion written all over his face.

I know what he's thinking, thought Fatimah: Two young Muslims come to make trouble.

Hassan approached him first. 'We've come to see Steve,' he said.

The policeman shook his head. 'I'm not allowed to let anyone in,' he said firmly.

Fatimah interrupted. 'Look, I'm Fatimah. I was the one who saved his life in the church.' She blushed as she said it, but they had to get into the house. And she could see that the policeman was looking at her differently now, so she pressed her advantage.

She gestured towards Hassan. 'And this is my brother,' she said. 'We've both been to the house before.'

Then she noticed a movement at the front window. Steve was waving at them. The next moment he was opening the door and limping down the path towards them.

'Quick,' he said. 'Come inside.'

The policeman frowned. 'I don't think you ...'

'They're my friends,' said Steve. 'I invited them over.'

But, when they were out of sight, the policeman made a phone call.

As soon as Hassan and Fatimah were in the house, Steve started to talk.

'Hey, calm down,' said Hassan. 'Start from the

beginning. You're going too fast.'

'Sorry,' said Steve. 'But there's not much time. I have to explain quickly.'

He showed them what he'd printed out from his computer. And he produced the numbers that Fatimah had given him and the outline of the crest. He explained what he thought it meant.

Fatimah's eyes widened. She looked across at Hassan. 'What do you think?' she said.

'Well ... it could be, I suppose. But then, the figures might mean something quite different.'

'103035,' repeated Fatimah.

Steve looked from one to the other. 'Look, I know it's a slim chance, but if I'm right, if there's any possibility it is what I think it is, then we must do something.'

Fatimah looked at her watch. '10.30 on 3rd May.'

Steve nodded. 'Exactly an hour and a quarter from now.'

'We must tell the police,' said Hassan.

Steve looked at Fatimah. 'What about your father? You didn't want him to know about the note.'

Fatimah flung up her hands in exasperation. 'For goodness sake, Steve! This is more important than what I want. We're talking about people's lives here!'

'Then I can ring them?'

'Of course. Get on with it.'

Quickly, Steve punched in the special number and waited. But after a few rings, the voicemail kicked in.

'Bloody hell! What do we do now?'

Fatimah looked out of the window. 'What about the guy out there?

'I don't think he's got any clout, but he'll have to do, I suppose.'

Hassan and Fatimah were out of the door and racing along the path before Steve had got his crutches tucked under his arm. He followed behind them. They were already talking to the policeman. As Steve caught up, they turned to him.

'He's been in touch with the guy in charge of the case. He's on his way.'

'Why?' asked Steve, frowning. 'Why did you contact him?'

The man's face showed no emotion. 'Procedure,' he said.

He means that he suspected Hassan and Fatimah, thought Steve. That's why he called the guy.

'Phone him again,' pleaded Steve. 'This can't wait.'

'He's on his way,' said the policeman calmly. 'He'll be here soon.'

It was the longest ten minutes in Steve's life. He checked his watch every few seconds and, when he wasn't doing that, he was staring down the road, willing the police car to come.

But when the car arrived, he was surprised. It was an unmarked car and there was only one man in it – the policeman who had been to see Steve and Fatimah in hospital. He wasn't wearing uniform.

He got slowly out of the car and smiled at them.

Steve started to gabble at him.

'Hey, slow down, Steve.'

Steve rummaged in his pocket and brought out the piece of paper with the numbers and the shield on it. Trying to speak calmly, he explained what he thought it meant and where it came from.

'I think it could be one of three buildings,' he said quickly, and he told the man which ones.

The policeman frowned. 'Why?'

Steve was in an agony of frustration. He tried to be patient. 'Because of the dates. They are all Victorian buildings; they were all built in 1885.'

The policeman said nothing. Steve went on. 'Please do something. Something's going to happen very soon – in less than an hour from now. Please believe me.'

'Wait,' said the policeman. He walked back to the car and spoke into the police radio.

'OK,' he said, 'I'll do what I can. You'd better come with me and we'll talk as I drive.'

Hassan and Fatimah helped Steve into the back

seat. It was awkward because his leg stuck straight out, but somehow, Hassan managed to squeeze himself in beside him and Fatimah sat in front. Steve leant forward as far as he could. Even in his anxiety, he was acutely conscious of Fatimah's body so close to his.

As they sped along the city streets, they answered the questions fired at them by the policeman.

'Why wasn't this note given to the police?' said the policeman, looking at Fatimah.

'Because it said I was a white boy's whore,' said Fatimah, clearly and without emotion, although she blushed as she said it. 'And I didn't want my father to know about it. And I had no idea it might be important,' she added.

Steve felt himself blushing, too. No wonder she didn't tell me what it said, he thought. Or her father.

The man nodded. Then he switched on the police radio and gave some terse commands. Steve listened carefully to the instructions he gave.

'Why are you so sure it's that building?' he asked.

'I'm not sure, Steve. But it's the most likely target.'

'Why?'

The man hesitated. 'There's a VIP there today. But I can't tell you any more.'

'Who knows about it?'

'Only a very few people.' The man frowned. 'It's been kept under wraps, so I don't know how the information can have got out.'

'Aren't the police there already, then?' said Hassan. 'Surely ...'

'Yes, it's swarming with police,' he said. 'Plain-clothes police all over the place. And it's already been searched from top to bottom.'

As they drove across the city, Steve became increasingly uneasy.

'Surely,' he whispered to Hassan, 'no one would try anything if they knew the place was full of police?'

'But where else could it be? It seems the obvious target, doesn't it?'

Steve looked at his watch. There was so little time left. He was exhausted from pain and lack of sleep and his mind was racing, trying to make connections with the other two buildings of exactly the same date – 1885 – that he'd found on the net. One was the Town Hall and the other a concert hall.

Suddenly Hassan clutched his arm. 'I've remembered something,' he whispered. He leaned nearer to Steve. 'When the imam and the vicar came to see us, weren't they saying something about a meeting between them and lots of other people – people of different faiths and backgrounds?'

Steve nodded. 'Yes, I vaguely remember something.'

'When?' said Hassan. 'Do you remember when

they said it was happening?'

Steve shook his head. 'They just said soon.'

Fatimah overheard and screwed her head round. 'Dad said he'd been invited to go to a meeting today,' she said, 'with the imam. Apparently it had been arranged for ages – before the church was bombed – but it's sort of snowballed since then and more people are being involved ...'

'When? Where?' Hassan was shouting and the policeman looked round.

'I don't know,' said Fatimah miserably. 'I'm sorry ... I just didn't listen ... I –'

Hassan grabbed her shoulders. 'Think! Did he say any more? Did he say where? At the mosque? At the Town Hall?'

She shook her head. Then she said quickly. 'I'll phone Mum. She might know.'

The policeman slowed right down. 'What's all this about?' he asked. Steve tried to explain while Fatimah phoned her mum. She chewed her lip anxiously as the phone rang and then spoke urgently as soon as her mother picked it up. The others held their breath until she snapped her mobile shut.

She turned frightened eyes on the two boys.

'It's at the Town Hall,' she said. 'And the meeting is at 10.15.'

'So, by 10.30 the bomber can be sure that everyone

has arrived,' muttered Hassan.

'I could be wrong ...' began Steve. But no one listened and, without a word, the policeman wrenched the steering wheel round and headed the car in the opposite direction. At the same time he was barking instructions once again into the police radio.

No one spoke. At one point it looked as though they were going to be stuck in traffic, but the policeman dived into the glove compartment of the car and pulled out a light. It had a magnetic base and he slammed it up on to the roof of the car and flicked a switch. Immediately the light began to flash and traffic moved aside to let them through.

All of them kept checking their watches. Ten o'clock had already passed and they still weren't there.

'We're going to be too late,' said Hassan.

'Don't worry, son,' said the policeman. 'I've told men to go in there straight away. They have instructions to clear the building.'

'Will they get there in time?' asked Fatimah. 'My father ...'

The policeman didn't answer. He was busy weaving his way through a narrow street, a short cut to the centre.

At last, they stopped.

'Why are you stopping here?' asked Steve.

'It's a good vantage point. We can see everything from here,' said the policeman. 'And I can give instructions. My people should be there any minute now.'

Steve saw Fatimah bow her head and place her hands on either side of her face.

She's praying, he thought. Even at this moment, when her father is in such danger, she's calm enough to pray.

Suddenly there was a crackle on the radio. The policeman tuned in.

'Damn!' he swore.

'What's happened?' asked Steve.

'They still haven't got there,' he said shortly.

'Hasn't someone told people at the Town Hall to clear the building?' asked Hassan.

'They've tried. Apparently the lines are all busy!'

'Then they must try again,' yelled Hassan. 'They must keep trying.'

They all got out of the car except the policeman, who was still talking into the radio, giving urgent instructions. Hassan helped Steve to struggle out of the back seat and handed him his crutches.

Fatimah looked up at the clock on the Town Hall. The hands were inching towards half past ten.

'Hassan, we must get inside. We must try and get Dad.'

She started to move forward but Hassan grabbed her arm. 'Don't be a fool,' he said roughly.

Then the policeman jumped out of the car and started to run. 'Stay here! I'm going in!' he yelled, as he headed towards the building, talking into a mobile as he ran.

They felt helpless as the seconds passed. Hassan and Fatimah were staring at the building, as if by doing so they might somehow avert the disaster.

'Perhaps I've got it wrong,' said Steve quietly. 'Perhaps it's got nothing to do with the meeting or the Town Hall...'

No one bothered to answer him. He looked round miserably. They were parked on a rise, beside an arcade. People were coming and going.

Then, at last, there was activity around the town hall. Police cars had arrived. People were shouting through loud-hailers.

'Don't let them be too late,' muttered Fatimah.

Steve shifted his weight. He felt dizzy. He put his head between his hands and shook it, trying to clear his thoughts.

And it was at that moment that he saw a movement, in the shadow behind one of the pillars of the arcade, just a few metres away. There was something about the quiet deliberation of the movement that attracted his attention. He stared at the young man standing there, almost obscured. He was just a boy, probably no older than Steve. And he was watching the clock.

In a moment of absolute clarity, Steve knew what the young man was going to do. He watched, horrified, as the boy reached into his pocket for a mobile phone, still with his eyes fixed on the town hall clock.

Steve made a split second decision. He couldn't reach him in time; he'd be too slow. He couldn't alert the others in time. He must do something. Slipping his crutch from under his arm, he hurled it towards the young man.

The crutch struck him on the arm. The young man staggered and fell, as the mobile flew from his hand and clattered on to the pavement.

'Get it!' shrieked Steve to Hassan. 'Get the mobile!'

Hassan dived for the mobile and snatched it up. The young man was struggling to his feet and made a grab at Hassan, trying to get the mobile back.

'Give it to me! I've got to do it! I've got to set it off!'

Their eyes met.

'Habib!'

Fatimah was staring at him, too.

'For Chrissake, switch it off!' yelled Steve at Hassan.

With trembling hands, Hassan switched off the mobile. Then he flung it violently to the ground and kicked it away.

Habib was standing there shaking, his head bowed. He sank down in a crumpled heap as Fatimah ran towards him. When she reached him, she grabbed his shoulders.

'How could you! How could you do this?'

'Who is he?' asked Steve.

Hassan swallowed. 'He's Aisha's brother Habib.'

'What! The girl who was killed? Fatimah's friend? But why?'

Hassan spread his hands in a gesture of helplessness. He couldn't speak.

Fatimah was shouting at Habib. 'My father is in there! You were going to kill him!'

But Habib just went on shaking his head to and fro.

Fatimah put her hand under his chin and yanked his face round, forcing him to look at her.

'How could you do this, Habib? After all your family's been through!'

Habib stared at her, uncomprehending. Then he started muttering, over and over, a sort of mantra:

'We must slay the unbelievers. Wherever they are, we must seek them out.'

'You're crazy,' said Hassan. 'Those are innocent

people in there.'

Habib shook his head again. 'Our teacher says …' he began.

'Who is your teacher?' said Hassan sharply. 'Who has been filling your head with this rubbish.'

Habib jerked his head up. 'It is not rubbish,' he said. 'It is not. How dare you say it is rubbish. You are as bad as the rest of them. You have no respect; you are not true followers of Islam.'

Fatimah sat back on her heels. She was shaking with rage but she forced herself to speak calmly. 'You know that is not true, Habib. You know that our family are good Muslims.'

For a few moments he stared back at her, a look of fury on his face, but then, as she held his gaze steadfastly, he bent his head and started to moan, 'I don't want to die. I don't want to die.'

Steve stood back, shocked. He turned to Hassan. 'Who has been brainwashing him?'

Hassan looked desperate. 'I don't know. He went abroad to visit family last year. I don't know if anyone got to him then …'

Habib raised his head. 'No!' he said violently. 'No, my teachers are here.'

'Teachers? Who are they?' asked Fatimah. 'Habib you must tell us. For your family's sake … for your mother's.'

She sat down beside Habib on the pavement. A passer-by asked if they were all right and Steve answered quickly, 'He just fell over. He's fine now.' As he said it, he noticed the policeman coming back towards the car.

Steve touched Hassan on the shoulder and pointed. 'What are we going to tell him?' he whispered.

They watched as the policeman raced up the hill towards them.

Steve thought quickly. 'Habib,' he said urgently. 'You've got to tell the police who they are, your teachers. You've got to tell the police.'

Habib wasn't listening to him. He was looking desperately at Fatimah.

He loves her, thought Steve. If anyone can get him to do what we ask, it is Fatimah. He'll do anything for her. I can see it in his eyes. He's crazy about her.

The policeman was beside them.

'Thank God we found it,' he said. 'We found the bomb. There was a mobile on it, but the bomb squad guys jammed the signal coming through this area.'

'So it can't be activated now?' said Steve.

The policeman shook his head. 'No. They'll take the bomb away and do a controlled explosion, then they'll unblock the signal.'

It was only then that he noticed Habib, still crouched on the ground.

'Who's this?'

Hassan said nothing. He bent down, picked up the mobile and handed it to the policeman.

Fatimah stood up and put out her hand to Habib. As she pulled him to his feet, his eyes never left her face.

'Habib,' she said. 'Tell the policeman everything you know.'

CHAPTER TWELVE

Habib's family were shattered. They'd lost their daughter and now they'd learnt that their son had been part of a terrorist group. A lot of people avoided them, not knowing what to say to them, how to react, and the family were now receiving hate mail and threatening phone calls, but Fatimah and Hassan and their parents went to see them often.

Auntie Leila looked terrible. Her eyes were swollen and she fiddled all the time with a sodden tissue in her hand. 'How could he?' she said, over and over. 'How could he believe what they told him? How could he believe that innocent people should die?'

Fatimah tried to be positive. 'Habib's helped the police a lot, Auntie,' she said. 'If it wasn't for him, those other men would still be free.'

'Yes,' added Hassan. 'And he stopped one of the others from attacking our house. And he had no idea that they were going to bomb the church, did he?'

Auntie Leila shook her head. 'Of course not.' She hesitated. 'After it happened, they told him that Aisha was a martyr and that she would go straight to Paradise.'

'I know,' said Fatimah gently.

'Nothing can excuse him,' said Leila, 'but he did try to leave the group after she died.'

'You can't leave that sort of group,' said Hassan.

Auntie Leila shook her head. 'They told him he must prove his loyalty. That's why they gave him the job of setting off the bomb at the Town Hall.'

'Poor Habib,' said Hassan.

Auntie Leila reached out for Fatimah's hand. 'Now I have no children with me,' she said. 'Aisha is dead and Habib is in police custody.'

'But he's not been charged with anything, has he?' asked Fatimah.

Leila sniffed. 'No. Not yet. But even if they release him, he'll never be the same again. He's so confused and miserable. He was so influenced by these people, so convinced they were right. And then his sister ...' She stopped for a moment to compose herself. 'And now, he sees what is happening to his family.'

Fatimah looked at Hassan. He nodded slightly.

'Auntie,' he said, 'perhaps you can help make things better.'

Six months after the church bombing. Fatimah, Hassan, Steve and their parents, the imam and the vicar, Auntie Leila and her family and lots of other people were all at a meeting. It was a large gathering and it was not the first time they had all come together, but it was the first time that they had gone public. This time, the television cameras were there and millions of viewers would see them. It wasn't comfortable and no one knew what the consequences might be.

Fatimah and Steve and their families sat on the platform at the end of the room, together with the vicar and the imam and some important people from the town.

There were several speeches – from the mayor, from the imam and the vicar – about how everyone living in the city needed to find ways to come together to fight terrorism and how they must break down prejudice and build up understanding.

Then the Press were invited to ask questions.

The first reporter stood up and asked Ben:

'You were pretty outspoken against Muslims when your son was injured. Are you really prepared to work with them now to help build these bridges?'

Steve and Jackie both held their breath, willing

Ben to find the right words.

'It won't be easy,' said Ben at last, 'but it seems to me that we have no choice. We are all British.' He turned to look at Jackie and she smiled with relief.

The next question was for Steve.

'Is there a romance between you and Fatimah, Steve?'

This made Steve really angry. Why were they still going on about this when something else so important was happening in this room? But he kept his cool, though he could feel the familiar blush rising to his cheeks.

'No,' he said slowly. 'No romance.' He paused, choosing his words carefully. 'But I respect her very much.'

Fatimah stood up. 'Ours will be a working relationship,' she said. 'We will work towards better understanding between our communities.' She hesitated and looked directly at Steve. 'We know there will be difficulties,' she said quietly, 'but then, nothing worthwhile is achieved without difficulties.'

Then, speaking more confidently, she looked at Auntie Leila, who was sitting in the front row of the hall with Habib beside her.

'And we have decided to dedicate our work to the memory of my best friend, Aisha.'

Auntie Leila sat very still, looking down at her

hands which were clasped in her lap. Slowly she raised her head to look at Fatimah and, as they held each other's eyes, the tears ran, unchecked, down Leila's cheeks.

Steve looked at Fatimah, too.

A working relationship? Well, there can be no other – can there?

But hang on, what had she just said?

He smiled to himself.

Nothing worthwhile is achieved without difficulties.

ROSEMARY HAYES
met up with a group of teenage
Muslim girls to learn more about their faith
and way of life after reading newspaper reports
about young, non-radical British Muslims who
want their voices heard. From these meetings
came the idea for the story of *Mixing It*.
Her first novel, *Race Against Time* (Puffin),
was runner-up for the Kathleen Fidler Award.
She has written a number of books for young
children including *The Gremlin Buster* (Puffin)
and *The Smell that Got Away* (Puffin), as well as
historical novels, adventure stories and a family saga
for older children. She is also a reader for a well
known authors' advisory service. Rosemary lives
and works in Cambridgeshire.

MORE FRANCES LINCOLN FICTION

GIVE ME SHELTER
STORIES ABOUT CHILDREN WHO SEEK ASYLUM

Edited by Tony Bradman

Sabine is escaping a civil war...
Danny doesn't want to be soldier...
What has happened to Samir's family?

Here is a collection of stories about children from
all over the world who must leave their homes and
families behind to seek a new life in a strange land.
Many are escaping war or persecution. All must
become asylum seekers in the free lands of the West.
If they do not escape, they will not survive.

These stories, some written by asylum seekers and
people who work closely with them, tell the story
of our humanity and the fight for the most basic
of our rights – to live. It is a testimony to all the people
in need of shelter and those from safer countries
who act with sympathy and understanding.

ISBN: 978-184507-571-2

REBEL CARGO

James Riordan
Introduced by Beaula Kay McCalla

Abena is an Ashanti girl sold into slavery
and transported on the notorious sea-route from
West Africa to Jamaica's sugar plantations.
Mungo is an English orphan who becomes a cabin boy,
only to be kidnapped and sold on as a white slave.
When fate brings the two youngsters together,
Mungo risks life and limb to save Abena from
a terrible death. Together they escape to the
Blue Mountains – where there is rumoured to be
a stronghold of runaways ruled by the legendary
leader Nanny. But can Mungo and Abena
get there before the Redcoats with their
baying bloodhounds drag them back...?

Based on events and records of the time, the novel
unflinchingly describes conditions of slavery
in the early 18th century – a time when
profits took precedence over humanity –
and ends on a note of hope.

ISBN: 978-184507-525-5

CHRISTOPHE'S STORY

Nicki Cornwell
Illustrated by Karin Littlewood

Christophe has a story inside him – and this story
wants to be told. But with a new country,
a new school and a new language to cope with,
Christophe can't find the right words. He wants
to tell the whole school about why he had to leave
Rwanda, why he has a bullet wound on his waist
and what happened to his baby brother, but has he
got the courage to be a storyteller? Christophe must
find a way to break through all these barriers,
so he can share his story with everyone.

ISBN 10: 1-84507-521-8

ISBN 13: 978-1-84507-521-7

GHADDAR THE GHOUL
AND OTHER PALESTINIAN STORIES

Sonia Nimr
Illustrated by Hannah Shaw
Introduced by Ghada Karmi

Why do Snakes eat Frogs?
What makes a Ghoul turn Vegetarian?
How can a Woman make a Bored Prince Smile?
The answers to these and many other questions
can be found in this delicious anthology of
Palestinian folk stories. A wry sense of humour
runs through the characterful women, genial
tricksters and mischievous animals who make
an appearance. Sonia Nimr's upbeat storytelling,
bubbling with wit and humour, will delight
readers discovering for the first time
the rich tradition of Palestinian storytelling.

ISBN: 978-1-84507-523-1

THE PRINCE WHO THOUGHT
HE WAS A ROOSTER
AND OTHER JEWISH STORIES

Ann Jungman
Illustrated by Sarah Adams
Introduced by Michael Rosen

A Chilli Champion... a Golem...
a Prince who thinks he's a Rooster?
Find them all in this collection of traditional
Jewish tales – lovingly treasured, retold and
carried through countries as far apart as Poland,
Afghanistan, Czechoslovakia, Morocco, Russia
and Germany, with a cast of eccentric princes,
sharp-witted scholars, flustered tailors and
the liveliest corpse of all! Seasoned with wit,
humour and magic, Ann Jungman's retellings
of stories familiar to Jewish readers are sure
to delight a new, wider readership.

ISBN: 978-184507-793-8